THEY CAME TO DEADWOOD

Tom Murcott—Part owner of the struggling Deadwood stage line, he staked his life and his fortune on stopping the deadly threat of the outlaw raiders.

Ellen Dorsey—On stage she could captivate an audience; in the rough, dusty streets of Deadwood she got caught in a deadly crossfire that would test her love and grit.

Wild Bill Hickok—He came to Deadwood to prospect, to gamble, and to be the target of a ruthless hired gun.

Calamity Jane—A wildcat who became a living legend, she kept one eye on Wild Bill Hickok, and the other on everybody else.

Johnny Varnes—Leader of the band of killers who preyed upon Deadwood, he terrorized Murcott's gold shipments, and would stop at nothing to eliminate his enemies.

The Stagecoach Series
Ask your bookseller for the books you have missed

STAGECOACH STATION 11:
DEADWOOD

Hank Mitchum

 Created by the producers of
Wagons West, White Indian,
and Saga of the Southwest.

Chairman of the Board: Lyle Kenyon Engel

BANTAM BOOKS
TORONTO · NEW YORK · LONDON · SYDNEY

STAGECOACH STATION 11: DEADWOOD

*A Bantam Book / published by arrangement with
Book Creations, Inc.*

Bantam edition / April 1984

*Produced by Book Creations, Inc.
Chairman of the Board: Lyle Kenyon Engel.*

ISBN 0-553-23998-8

Published simultaneously in the United States and Canada

PRINTED IN THE UNITED STATES OF AMERICA

H   0 9 8 7 6 5 4 3 2 1

Author's Note

Although this book is a work of fiction, many incidents really happened and many of the characters existed. Such have been depicted with as much historical accuracy as possible, given the wide-ranging and often conflicting published accounts of Deadwood in 1876.

Foremost among the historical characters who walk through the pages of this story are James Butler "Wild Bill" Hickok and Martha "Calamity Jane" Canary. Their characterizations closely follow the written accounts of those who knew them best, unlike the romanticized portrayals of the past.

Also on the list of historical figures who play a role in this novel are Jack Langrishe—whose theater hall was used for the trial of Jack McCall—and gambler Johnny Varnes, as well as the minor characters William Kuykendall, Carl Mann, Bill Massie, Charlie Rich, Billy Nuttall, Steve Utter, and Colorado Charlie Utter.

STAGECOACH STATION 11:

DEADWOOD

Chapter 1

The heavy rains these first two weeks of July 1876 had done the stage road through the Black Hills of Dakota Territory no good at all. It was a makeshift road, hacked out over impossible grades, with tree stumps still standing to catch and smash a wheel under an unwary stagecoach driver. For now, at least, the rain seemed to be over, leaving behind the steaming earth and a thin, silver mist caught in the branches of the tall pines overhead.

It also left new dangers—slick stretches where a coach could slew about without warning, and bottomless mud that could swallow wheels to the hubs if the driver let his four-horse team lose momentum. Tom Murdock knew he didn't have to worry about his driver, Farley Haymes; still, there were moments when he knew the half-dozen passengers inside were clinging to their seats.

Up on the forward boot with legs braced and loaded rifle ready across his knees, he scarcely noticed Farley Haymes swearing and yelling at his tough, trailwise animals. Murdock's whole attention was on the shouldering rock and timber and the brushy reaches in between, his keen stare constantly searching out likely spots for ambush. If there were another robbery of a shipment of gold dust, the stage line Murdock owned with two other men might go under, and he did not intend to let that happen.

For the first twenty-eight years of his life Tom Murdock had worked for other people. Until he was nineteen the muscular boy had worked on his family's farm in Maine, and he had stayed there during the war, laboring on the land while his older brother, Sam, took off to fight— experiencing the excitement and adventure that Tom se-

1

cretly craved. But someone had been needed to maintain the farm, since their parents were dead. After the war, Sam married and wanted to buy Tom's share of the farm for himself. Tom had moved on, deciding that he could no longer live in his brother's shadow.

The West had offered Tom Murdock the distance from his home that he needed and the adventure he desired. When the tall, sandy-haired young man with the deep voice and steady brown eyes had walked in to George Faraday's stage-line office in Oregon nine years ago and asked for a job, the owner felt he was a man to be trusted and hired him on the spot.

For almost seven years the two men had worked together compatibly, Murdock proving to be as reliable as Faraday had expected and as hard-working as his muscular build implied. Then, when the panic of seventy-three wiped out the business, Murdock for three years had wandered from settlement to settlement, doing whatever work he could find. When Faraday got the Deadwood Stage Line going last spring, he offered his former employee a one-third partnership. Murdock was more than ready to accept and commit himself and his money to the stage line's success.

He was a deliberate-speaking, quiet man who liked to avoid violence when possible. But pushed too far, Murdock was a man to be reckoned with—a man positive of his actions.

And now he was not going to let some gold-hungry outlaws ruin what he had worked so hard to establish.

Murdock squinted his eyes and continued to scan the dense forest bordering the road. It was a total of fifty-odd miles from Deadwood south to Custer City. They had covered a little less than half that distance so far on this run without any sign of trouble.

From his seat on the coach roof, the field agent for Murdock's stage line, Polk Renner, was keeping his own vigil. Leaning forward to make himself heard, he now asked, "Do you fellows begin to get the notion we could be a tad overmanned for this operation?"

"Is that what you think?" Tom Murdock said.

"I'm kind of beginning to. Close to four hours since leaving Deadwood, and still nothing's happened." Polk Renner was a man whose age was hard to determine. His tightly curled brown hair and full mustache were peppered with gray, and the weather-blackened skin of his cheeks was marked with a fan of paler creases at the corners of eyes long accustomed to squinting in the sun. "Have they ever waited to hit a coach this far from camp, Farley?"

"Not as I recall," the driver admitted, eyes on the bobbing heads of his lead horses, lantern jaw distended by the wad of tobacco stuck into his cheek. "Still, how do we know but what some fresh talent may have moved into the neighborhood and are laying for us just this side of Custer, just waiting for their chance at a box full of gold dust?"

"Tom?" Polk Renner appealed to his boss. "What do *you* say?"

Murdock hesitated. "All we know for sure," he said finally, his deep voice slowly delivering his well-considered words, "is that the gold camps have got these hills crawling with outlaws. The Deadwood crowd we've had our eyes on don't have to be the only ones interested in our shipments. I, for one, don't figure we should relax till we reach Custer and have this load safely off our hands." He kicked a bootheel against the solid bulk of the chest that rode in the space beneath the driver's box.

"Nobody mentioned relaxing," Renner said gruffly.

The talk fell off, transformed into the silence of men who use words sparingly. By now the July sun had burned away most of the mist, and the narrow, dark trunks of the virgin timber seemed to sop up the light, giving this thickly grown, steep country its somber appearance. Murdock often thought it was little wonder that the Sioux, awed by the dark beauty of the region, had named it their sacred land—their Paha Sapa. In the more prosaic tongue of the white men who had usurped it, it was called the Black Hills. . . .

The road climbed a sharp rise and at the knife-edge crest took a sharp hook to the left as it started down the other side. A man who was unfamiliar with the route could have missed that turn and gone piling into a jumble of boulders, but Farley Haymes knew every twist and bend. He took this one adeptly, riding the brake and using the ribbons to ease his team into the descent. Anyone less familiar than Murdock with the fine points of handling a stage team might have been fooled into thinking the maneuver was a simple one—Haymes had done it easily. Murdock, knowing Haymes was embarrassed by any word of compliment, kept his appreciation to himself.

Moments later, at another twist of the road, Murdock heard the driver curse. Then Haymes was tromping the brake, roaring at his animals as he halted them with a strong and steady pull. In the same instant Tom Murdock saw the problem: A tree was down just ahead of them, right across the road—completely blocking it. After their rush down the slope, the lead horses could easily have plowed into the obstacle, causing a pileup and instant chaos for the stage and everybody aboard—which, Murdock was thinking, had been the whole intention of the ones responsible for dropping the tree. With reactions just as swift as his driver's, he now had the rifle ready and a shell jacked in place under the hammer. His alert eyes roved the trailside growth.

Without checking, Murdock knew Polk Renner was aware of their danger and had thrown himself flat against the stage roof, rolled onto his belly, and placed his rifle muzzle across the baggage rail on the opposite side. Neither man had long to wait. Riders with weapons in their hands came bursting out of the timber toward the stalled coach. As Murdock drew a bead on the leader, he heard the bang of Renner's gun, telling him the bushwackers were coming from both directions. He fired, and his shot echoed Renner's.

The attackers probably hadn't looked for such quick resistance; it must have come as quite a surprise. Murdock saw the flash of a pistol, and a bullet clipped the wooden panel where he had rested his arm for support. More shots slammed into the stage. He fired, levered, and fired again, holding steady against the recoil so that the rifle barrel would not be thrown off target. He saw the leader's horse toss its head and go crashing into a clump of bushes: It had taken a bullet meant for its rider. The man leaped clear, but when he fell, he lay as though stunned.

A pair of attackers who followed close behind the shot animal had to pull rein fast to avoid colliding, and as they steered their mounts around the fallen horse, one of Murdock's bullets split the air between them. Fighting their horses down, the ambushers shot back.

But now, guns were opening fire from the windows of the coach itself. Murdock recalled that two of his passengers had had the look of prospectors, carrying on board sacks that bulged with gold dust. Such men wouldn't hesitate to fight to protect their property. What must have seemed like an easy pick-off to the highwaymen who had felled the tree, stopping the Deadwood stage, had suddenly turned into something very different.

The barrel of Murdock's rifle was starting to grow warm, and now he saw that the bandits were retreating into the timber. In that moment a ray of sunlight fell across the face of one outlaw, striking the sheen of scar tissue. In some past knife fight a blade had glanced down the man's forehead, by some miracle missing his eye, and sliced across the flesh of the cheekbone. Below that, the puckered scar disappeared beneath the bandanna that covered the rest of his face. Murdock had only the one glimpse, but it was enough—he wasn't likely to forget that scar. An instant later the shadows of the timber hid it, and at the same time he heard Polk Renner shout above the racket, "Hey! My pair seems to have pulled out."

"Then cover me!" Tom Murdock ordered.

He dropped his smoking rifle onto the seat, stepped to the hub of the big wheel, and from there dropped to the ground. Laying a hand on a windowsill, he spoke to the men inside. "How about a couple of you lending me a hand?" He didn't have to ask twice. The door burst open and two hardy-looking passengers scrambled out. As Murdock, keeping low, turned to run past the frightened stage horses to the fallen tree, the two followed.

The bandits had picked a tree they could drop with a minimum of ax work. For three men it was no great chore to lay hold of one end, lift it, and swing it aside like a gate. There was renewed gunfire as the bandits saw their quarry about to escape, but Polk Renner and the remaining passengers fired back, making it difficult for any returned shots to be accurate. If the attackers thought belatedly of dropping one of the horses, they had lost their chance, for as soon as the road was clear, Farley Haymes yelled his teams into the harness, and the crack of his whip goaded them like a spur.

The stage leaped forward, the open door swinging wildly on its hinges. The two passengers managed to scramble inside, and Murdock slammed the door behind them. He leaped onto the iron step and, hooking an arm around the door frame, brought up his holster gun. As the stage horses fell into a steady run, two riders suddenly dropped into the road behind and came on, spurring hard. Murdock threw back a shot that was joined by such a barrage from the roof and windows of the coach that the pursuers reined up. Very quickly the pair were left behind—a picture of anger and frustration—and the twists of the road swallowed them up.

One, Murdock knew, was the man with the scar.

He looked in through the window, made sure none of the passengers were hurt, and said, "Well, we lost them. Thanks for the help." Afterward, catching at the baggage rail, he hoisted himself up to stand on the windowsill and from there climbed to the top of the coach, where he sprawled out alongside Polk Renner.

The first thing he saw was the blood that had soaked a large spot of red into the sleeve of his friend's shirt. "You caught one!" he exclaimed.

Renner shrugged. "It don't amount to nothing. Just a little, no-account bullet burn is all."

"It's the little ones that you bleed to death from, sometimes. Let me look at it." They braced themselves against the pitch and roll of the stage while Murdock made a quick examination. He tore off Renner's sleeve, ripped it up, and made a rough bandage, saying, "You appear to be right—it doesn't amount to much. Anderson's is the next stop. This will hold you until we get there and have it tended to proper." Looking at the road behind them, he added, "Looks like we made it through *that* piece of trouble."

The horses were still excited, blowing and tossing their heads while Farley Haymes swore at them affectionately, trying to calm them down. Murdock was about to return to his place beside the driver when Renner caught his arm to detain him. The pain he wouldn't admit to was in his voice as he demanded, "Did you see him?"

"The scar?" Murdock nodded. "It looked just as you described it."

"Oh, it was him, all right—no question. Whoever the bastard is, even wearing a mask he's got a face nobody'd be apt to forget. Which means," he added, "we know one thing for sure: This was part of the same crowd we've been having trouble with up around Deadwood. Question is, why did they ride an extra twenty miles out of their way this time before they hit us?"

Tom Murdock wiped his brow with an arm. "It just could be that whoever's doing their thinking figured it as a way to throw us off—set us to looking for new enemies and maybe lose sight of what's right under our noses."

"Well, if that was it, they spoiled their play when they let us have that look at ol' Scarface. He gave the whole game away." Polk Renner winced as the erratic sway of the coach jostled his injured arm against the roof. He showed his teeth in a ferocious grin. "By damn, it makes me real pleased to have them go to all that extra effort, only to have it come to nothing at all. . . ."

Chapter 2

Up until General Custer's Black Hills expedition of 1874, which confirmed the widespread belief that there was gold to be found there, scarcely a white man had dared to set foot in the sacred lands of the Sioux Indians. Inevitably, after the news of Custer's findings had broken the dam, a flood of fortune hunters poured illegally into what was still a Sioux reservation. The white intruders fanned out along every stream, their gold pans ready, and camps sprang up wherever the faintest glitter was found. Most of these places would quickly die and vanish; only a very few would live.

It was at one of these surviving camps that the south-bound coach arrived toward midday, dropping into a shallow basin that was ringed by rough and timbered hills. No one had bothered to give the settlement a name. It was generally referred to as Anderson's, after the man who had built a store there to accommodate the two or three hundred miners who worked their placer claims along the creeks nearby. For a monthly fee, Anderson allowed the stage line to use his log buildings as one of its stations and to keep replacement horses in his corral.

Farley Haymes brought his rig in toward the muddy work area in front of a few crude, wood-shingled buildings, where smoke from a mud chimney raveled out into the noontime stillness. Another stage was here ahead of them; a man with a tar bucket and swab was at work greasing one of the big rear wheels. This was the regular north-bound stage, which had left Custer City that morning. Barring accidents, the coaches from Custer and Deadwood generally met here at Anderson's, the halfway point, in their regular, three-times-a-week run.

"Sam Pryor appears to have himself a considerable load this trip," Haymes commented, indicating the stacks of crates and luggage lashed in place atop the other coach.

"It's that kind of business keeps us on the road," Murdock said dryly.

"I'll have to tell him to keep his eyes open. Wouldn't want him running into the same trouble we did."

"They'll probably leave him alone. He hasn't got anything they want."

"They don't necessarily know that. . . ."

As the southbound stage pulled up, Sam Pryor, who had been supervising the greasing job, came walking over. Pryor was a hairy, red-bearded young fellow with a wild look about him, but actually he was coolheaded and thoroughly efficient on the box of a Concord coach. He and Haymes did most of the driving for the company, shuttling passengers and freight between Deadwood and Custer City, where connections could be made with the stage from Cheyenne.

Farley Haymes's passengers piled out, full of talk about the attempted holdup, but Murdock was more concerned about Polk Renner. While the drivers talked matters over, Murdock tossed down his rifle to the stockman with instructions to watch the coach and make sure no one got near the strongbox; after that he helped Renner down. The man was in more pain from his bullet-torn arm than he wanted to let on, Tom Murdock thought as he walked his injured friend over to the log building. As they neared it, Murdock became aware of excited voices within that grew louder by the second.

Two months ago, when his store began to do extra service as a stage stop, Carl Anderson had found room for a couple of tables and had installed a rudimentary kitchen in the back, making it possible to provide meals of a sort. Just now, Murdock noticed, it looked as though Anderson's facilities were crammed to the limit. Several people, one of them a little girl, were seated at the tables with half-finished meals in front of them, but at the moment, not one of these customers—the passengers from Custer City, Murdock surmised—seemed much interested in eating.

They were all staring at the newcomers, who were talking loudly and interrupting one another as they competed to give a report of the attempted holdup. Anderson, a big-boned, sandy-haired man with a constantly worried expression, was trying to quiet them down and get answers to some direct questions. Suddenly all talk ceased as Tom Murdock entered and they saw the bloodstained bandage on the arm of the man beside him.

Into the sudden stillness Carl Anderson said heavily, "Maybe now a man can hear himself think! *You* tell us about it, Tom. What happened?"

"Whatever they told you is probably right," he answered. Murdock was not one for unnecessary speeches. "Somebody tried to rob the coach, but we had other ideas about it."

Anderson looked at Polk Renner. "How bad is he hurt?"

"I ain't hurt at all," Renner insisted indignantly, but without much conviction.

The storekeeper stepped up and took hold of Renner's injured arm. "Just give me a chance to look at that, so we can see what needs to be done. Meanwhile," he told the others, with a nod toward Murdock, "this here is Tom Murdock—he owns the stage line you folks have been riding with." Then, addressing one of the men at the tables, he said, "He'd be the one for you to talk to. He's from Deadwood, and he can tell you a lot more about the place than I can. . . . Polk, that arm of yours needs looking at. Come back to the kitchen and I'll see what I can do."

As they started for the kitchen, Renner still protesting, a middle-aged woman quickly got to her feet, declaring, "I think you'd best wait for me. You men are too heavy-handed to deal with a thing like this." She didn't wait for an invitation but went hurrying after them. She was competent looking and had what struck Murdock as a merry, friendly manner. He thought the little girl, who had been seated next to her at the table, might be the woman's daughter.

The man Anderson had spoken to got up from his place and came forward now with a smile and an extended hand. "How do you do?" he said to Murdock. The timbre of his voice suggested that if the man were to let it out, it could very well rattle the shingles on the roof overhead. "So you are the owner of the stage company?"

"Co-owner," Murdock corrected him, "along with my two partners—and there's a couple of banks that have something to say about it, too. You have a complaint to make?"

"What? Oh, no! Nothing like that." The man waved the thought aside. There was something in the way he moved—in every gesture, however small—that seemed at once to catch the eye. Somewhere in his mid-forties, the man was not large but was inclining toward pudginess. He had a round head—which was only fringed with dark hair—a beak of a nose, quick eyes, and a broad mouth. His meticulous way of dressing, the erect manner in which he held himself, and the lively intelligence in his glance made an instant impression.

"No complaints at all!" the man continued. "Aside from the fact that this is the third stagecoach my people and I have been compelled to travel in since leaving Denver. Naturally, the sooner we reach our destination, the happier we're all going to be."

"All of you are together?" Murdock saw that the still-seated travelers were watching and listening with apparent interest. A growing puzzlement suddenly made him tell the man, "You know, your face is mighty familiar. I would swear I'd seen you before."

"Well, it wouldn't have been around here," the man said, smiling. "Actually, I've hardly been outside of Colorado for something like—good Lord, has it actually been seventeen years?" He added, "The name is Langrishe. . . ."

Murdock repeated it, and then the truth struck him. "Langrishe! You're *Jack* Langrishe—you're the actor!"

The man seemed pleased. "Then you've heard of me? All the way up here?"

"The fact is, I saw you once. It was at a theater in Denver, maybe two years ago."

"Indeed?"

"You were Julius Caesar, and I thought you were great—even if I couldn't exactly make out the meaning of everything you said. No offense," he added quickly.

Langrishe's quick smile appeared again. Obviously not at all put out, he said blandly, "That's the beauty of playing Shakespeare: The sound gives the sense. It doesn't matter if you miss a few of the words. You surely don't suppose that, even in the Great Bard's day, the groundlings at the Globe Theatre always understood what the devil was going on? Here on the frontier, even when audiences can't follow the plot, they eat up the gestures—not to mention the costumes."

"And I take it these are the rest of your company?" Now that Murdock looked at them more closely, it seemed he should have known there was something special about these people. He noticed a remarkably beautiful woman and two unusually handsome young men. Of the others, one or two were ugly in an interestingly individual fashion. Each bore himself as though expecting to be looked at—features in repose and bodies poised as though trained to habitual control of gesture and movement. Anyone who had ever watched an actor upon a stage should have spotted them for what they were.

In answer to the question, Jack Langrishe said, "These are most of us. The woman who left a moment ago to offer her help to your friend was Mrs. Bertie Clevenger—my wardrobe mistress and one of the finest character actresses I've had the pleasure of working with."

"She didn't have to bother herself over Polk Renner."

"Oh, but that's her style! We've all learned that in any kind of emergency—from a broken arm to a hangnail—Bertie Clevenger is the person one goes to. She reacts to the sight of pain like a warhorse sniffing the smoke of battle!" Langrishe chuckled, then added, "My wife is still in Denver, closing out some personal matters; she'll join us when she can. And two of the male members are on the road behind us, with a wagon full of costumes and scenery."

"You seem to have pulled up stakes, for fair," Tom Murdock observed.

"I'll tell you how it is," Jack Langrishe said earnestly. "For seventeen years—ever since the first strikes back in fifty-nine—I've made a name for myself and my company by playing the mining camps, all through Colorado. Now, from what I hear of these Black Hills, this one sounds like the biggest strike of all. I'd had the feeling I should begin to look for new fields, and I decided the thing to do was to get in at the beginning of this one."

"Well, you'll be doing that, all right, if you come to Deadwood. Six months ago the place didn't even exist."

"And today?"

"Today, we're booming! No one can say for sure, but there could be two, maybe three thousand miners crowded into the camps along that gulch; the one called Deadwood is only the biggest. We got a couple hundred buildings, lots of tents, all kinds of businesses—hotels, a newspaper, a grocery, a bakery—and more than enough saloons," Murdock added dryly.

"Is there a theater?" Langrishe asked quickly.

"No, not really. One or two of the dance halls have stages of a sort, where the girls put on what passes for entertainment when they aren't busy working the customers. That's about as close as we come."

"I've been hoping to put up an auditorium."

"You won't find much space that doesn't have a building or a placer claim on it," Murdock said. "But you can look around. I'll be wishing you the best of luck."

Langrishe made a gesture that could only be termed a flourish as he intoned, "On behalf of all of us, I thank you. And also for the information . . ."

Murdock started toward the kitchen to check on Polk Renner's injury. At the crude plank counter that also served as a bar, his passengers were still discussing the holdup attempt with Anderson over tin cups filled from his whiskey jug. Not pausing, Murdock reminded them, "I suggest you put some food in your bellies on top of that stuff to settle it. You won't be getting another chance before we unload at Custer this evening." He was speaking over his shoulder, and as he reached the kitchen door, he had to make a hasty side step when he almost collided with a woman coming through.

She was young and more than just a little attractive. She wasn't tall, but she carried herself erectly. Her brown hair was swept back from her forehead to a tumble of curls; her eyes were blue, and they sparkled with intelligence and friendliness. She was smiling—whether at his clumsiness or just from general good feeling, he preferred not to guess.

"Sorry," he muttered, remembering to reach for his hat brim.

A dimple formed as her smile widened, and she nodded and went on past him. That was when he noticed she had a dishtowel tied around her waist for an apron and that she carried a tray. His look followed her as she went to one of the tables and began picking up dirty dishes. Then, because he felt foolish staring, he shook his head and passed through the door into the kitchen, reminding himself that he was going to have to ask Carl Anderson about this employee.

In the kitchen Polk Renner was seated at the table, scowling and grumbling. Bertie Clevenger was busy with cloth and scissors, fixing a neat bandage. The portly woman's movements were deft and gentle, her features and soothing words full of concern. Murdock suspected that for all his gruff manner, Polk Renner was really eating up the attention.

"You going to be able to travel again?" Murdock asked him.

"Oh, hell, yes—excuse me, ma'am," Renner added to Bertie. "Whenever you are, Tom. I keep telling people I ain't really hurt, but I can't get nobody to believe me."

Over his head, Bertie Clevenger looked at Murdock and clucked her tongue reprovingly. "Don't let him fool you. Some men just don't have good sense when it comes to admitting they aren't made of cast iron. Next thing you know, some piffling little thing happens and they fall right on their faces!" She added with severity, "Now, will you stop squirming, Mr. Renner, and let me finish here?"

"And after that, Polk," Tom Murdock told him in his deep voice, "you'd best get yourself something to eat and be ready to leave when this coach pulls out for Deadwood."

"Deadwood?" Renner protested. "Hey! I came with *you*, remember? And we're headed for Custer City."

"*I* am—you're not. Change of plan," Murdock explained briefly. "The other coach isn't carrying any guard. With all these people aboard, I'd feel better knowing you're sitting up on the boot alongside Sam Pryor."

"You mean, in case we run into Scarface again," Renner finished for him. "All right. You're the boss."

If Bertie Clevenger understood or was disturbed by what they were saying, she didn't let on. Lips pursed and head to one side, she finished tying off the bandage on Polk Renner's arm.

The lovely young brown-haired woman came back then, carrying a tray heaped with dirty dishes. Tom Murdock watched her place her tray on the drainboard, and then with movements that were swift and graceful even at this menial task, she began scraping the plates into a bucket at her feet, afterward stacking the dishes in a sink. He had an idea she knew he was observing her, and that made him self-conscious. Finally he spoke, his voice gravelly from shyness, "Ma'am, you're new here, aren't you? I never heard about Anderson taking on a hired girl."

That brought her head around, and she grinned with amusement at his mistake. "He hasn't. With so many of us piling in on him like this, I thought it only right to chip in and lend a hand."

"That's our Ellen for you, Mr. Murdock," Bertie Clevenger said. "A body can always count on her stepping in to help."

Murdock looked from one woman to the other. To Ellen he said, "Is she telling me you're a part of the company? Are you an actress, too?"

"An actress?" She stopped and repeated the word, frowning thoughtfully. Then her smile was back as she answered, "I don't suppose anybody really knows yet."

"Now, what would that mean?"

She had taken a steaming kettle off the big wood-burning range and was pouring hot water over the dishes when Carl Anderson came striding in. One look and he exclaimed in horror, "Lady—*no!* I appreciate your helping, but I won't have you doing my dishes for me. Now you take that apron off." He caught the look on Murdock's face then and read it correctly. With amusement plucking at the corner of his mouth, he added, "Besides, here's Tom Murdock working up a lather and dying to have a talk with you."

"What?" Suddenly shy, Ellen glanced quickly at Murdock. Then she looked at him again, more directly, and as though on impulse, she smiled and took the towel from around her waist, dried her hands on it, and laid it aside. "All right. Perhaps," she suggested tentatively, "we could step outside—get ourselves some fresh air."

"Good idea," Murdock said approvingly. He indicated the main room, which was busy now with a jumble of many voices. "It's getting pretty noisy in here. . . ."

The rear entrance opened directly onto a sweep of the valley floor that, from here, showed few signs yet of the drastic changes the white man had brought to this country. Murdock and the woman picked their way past a few boxes of trash and empty bottles and, a little way from the building, found a shaded place beneath a spreading pine. From there they could see the dusty ribbon of the stage road curling up into the dark timber, and elsewhere untouched grass shining in the sunlight—the cup of hills lying silent and without motion under the stillness of midday.

He watched her lift her head and breathe deeply of the pine scent that hung about them. "You seem to like this country," he said after a minute, his deep voice softer now but still resonant.

She looked at him and smiled. "It's beautiful! So different from anything I ever knew."

"I've never seen any place quite like the Black Hills, myself," Murdock conceded. "Just where are you from, Miss—"

"It's Dorsey—Ellen Dorsey. And I was born in a little

town in Indiana, one you never would have heard of. This is my very first time away from home."

"Then it *is* a new experience—in more ways than one, I bet. What was it you meant back there, about not knowing whether you're an actress?"

"Just what I said. . . ." When she saw the real interest in his look, she took a breath and went on—almost as though it would be a relief to unburden to someone, even a stranger. "It's all happened so fast. I arrived in Cheyenne only a few days ago. My mother passed away very suddenly and left me all alone. My father—well, he's supposed to be a salesman, though I suppose almost anyone would be more apt to call him a drifter. It's been a long time since I've seen him, but I loved him very much when I was little. We heard from him from time to time, and he sent us money on occasion when he had some or thought about it. . . . Mother and I did sewing and things like that to help make up the difference.

"With Mother gone, all at once I didn't have anybody, and I felt lost and alone. The last place I heard from Pa was Cheyenne, and I had some reason to think he might still be there. I sent him a wire but got no answer. Finally, on the chance of finding him, I used almost the last of my money for a train ticket. Well, I suppose you've guessed that he was gone when I arrived—drifted on again, and not a clue as to where. So I had to give him up. And there I was, alone and broke. Nobody was hiring any seamstresses."

"All that on your first time away from home," Tom Murdock said, "and in a town like Cheyenne. . . . Weren't you scared?"

She admitted it freely. "I was terrified! I didn't know which way to turn. Then I happened to hear that a theater troupe had arrived in town on their way from Colorado to Dakota Territory and that they were looking for someone who could play young girls' parts and do some singing. I'd never been on a stage, but back home I used to sing in church and at weddings. Anyway, I was desperate enough that I went to see Mr. Langrishe and audition for him—and I guess he was desperate enough to hire me! It turned

out that someone had suddenly quit and left the company—
I think she may have heard some things about the Black
Hills she didn't like the sound of.

"Mr. Langrishe told me"—she looked embarrassed as
she repeated it—"that he could easily have got one of the
girls from those Cheyenne dance halls, only he wouldn't
hire such people. I seemed to be the type he needed. He
liked my voice well enough, and he had me read a couple
of scenes. I thought I was really dreadful, but he hired me
on the spot. And—well, here I am!"

She said this with a toss of her head and a flash of her
smile. Murdock decided, with admiration, that whether
she could act or not, this lady was certainly game, ready to
make the best of any situation she found herself in.

"I bet you're going to be just fine," he said. "I only
hope I get a chance to see you."

"But I thought I heard your friend telling Bertie that
you live in Deadwood."

"Only in a manner of speaking. That's where our
headquarters are, but I'm on the road a lot. Our stage line
is more or less just getting started," he explained. He
shifted his weight from one foot to the other and ran a
hand through his hair. "One of my partners runs the
office, and the other stays out in the field, drumming up
business and credit. My job is to see that the stages keep
rolling, so I'm not in town all that much. Right now I have
a strongbox of dust to be turned over to the Cheyenne
stage, down at Custer."

"Dust?" She looked puzzled.

"Gold dust," he explained, and he saw her eyes widen.
"So in a few minutes I'm afraid you and I will be heading
in opposite directions. I sure hope the rest of your trip
goes well, and that you find everything to your liking at
Deadwood. Once I know when your opening performance
is, I'll make it a point to be there, if I can, and give you a
big hand."

Ellen Dorsey's eyes clouded. "I don't know that I
want you to be there. These other folks are all true
performers, and I'm only an amateur. I'm really scared."

"I'll be there," he said with a shy smile. "And you mustn't worry."

There were things she *could* worry about, he thought bleakly as they turned and walked together back to the store—things that her predecessor had probably heard that had scared her out of trusting her luck in such a lawless place as Deadwood. But he kept the thought to himself—Ellen plainly had had no choice other than the one she had made. Fortunately, she had the rest of the acting company to give her protection and support. It would probably be best for Ellen Dorsey to find out in her own good time just what she was letting herself in for. . . .

Chapter 3

The Langrishe troupe filled the coach to overflowing, just as they had earlier filled the one that brought them from Cheyenne. Nine persons were sitting inside, and a couple more were riding the roof, which was otherwise loaded with boxes of freight and luggage. Polk Renner—seemingly now little the worse for the injury to his left arm—had taken a place beside the driver, a rifle propped within handy reach. Ellen Dorsey was relieved to know he was up there, guarding them. Word of this morning's attack on the southbound coach, somewhere along the same stretch of road they were traveling now, had been sobering for everyone.

Only three days had elapsed since she had joined this company, and Ellen still felt as troubled and out of place as she had been when they had boarded the coach that first morning at Cheyenne. As she stared out of the window as the coach bounced along the twisting, rutted road through the Black Hills, she thought back to those first uncomfortable hours as a member of the Langrishe acting company.

When the troupe had boarded the stage in Cheyenne, Ellen had found a place for herself on the leather-padded center board, which was inserted for use, along with a backrest suspended from the ceiling, whenever there were to be more than six inside passengers. Ellen, as the newest member of the troupe, never questioned that the better seats belonged by right of seniority to the others. This one proved as uncomfortable as she'd imagined, and it confronted her with the problem of trying to keep her knees from bumping those of the person facing her.

Nevertheless, she smilingly refused to trade places with Bruce Walker when he urged her to change with him, and in the end he gallantly gave up his own place and came over to sit beside her.

"You aren't being hard to get acquainted with, are you?" he said reprovingly but with a smile. "We just can't have that. You're part of the company now. We'll be traveling together, working together—under all kinds of conditions. Do you think it's right to be standoffish?"

She was taken aback. "Of course not! I'm—I'm sorry," she said, stammering, and a little angry with herself for doing it. "I didn't intend anything like that. But—you must see that a person might be a little shy, thrown in with so many new faces all at once. I don't even know all your names."

"Then that's something we'll have to take care of!" And he proceeded to introduce her to those she had not yet met.

Ellen found all the actors fascinating, from the Hamiltons—an elderly couple, both character players, with a vivacity and eagerness for life that had scarcely been dulled by their long years at a hard profession—to Claire Richards, the leading lady of the troupe, a dark-haired beauty who seemed to Ellen the loveliest woman she had ever set eyes on.

But the one who intrigued her the most was Bruce Walker himself. Strikingly good-looking, with blond hair worn long in the theatrical manner, he had charm and a deft, easygoing way about him that put her immediately at her ease. Earlier, in telling her something about the people she would be working with, Jack Langrishe had spoken at some length about Walker: "He could be a matinee idol on the New York stage if he wanted to. He certainly has the looks for it, and for that reason I usually have him playing leads. But when I can, I put him into more demanding roles because I consider him capable of far more challenging things. I'd like nothing better than to cast him in *Richard III*, but I've never been able to interest him in working on it. Too much trouble, I'm afraid. Too many lines to learn. . . ." Langrishe had shaken his head with a sigh. "I only wish he would take our profession more seriously."

Now that Ellen and Bruce Walker had traveled together, swaying and conversing pleasantly on that uncomfortable center bench, Ellen suspected that Langrishe was doomed to go on being disappointed. She gathered that acting on a stage was no more than a lark to Bruce Walker—a pleasant and undemanding way to make a passable living that left him with time and high energy for the more important enjoyment of living itself. In this he was the complete opposite of the grimly determined people who had surrounded her as she was growing up. She supposed she ought to disapprove, but instead she found his lighthearted charm almost irresistible.

Those last hours of the long journey from Cheyenne drew to an end, lightened—even made close to enjoyable— by Bruce Walker's entertaining presence. But now the things Ellen saw through the coach window appalled and amazed her.

She thought she had known what to expect. Entering the Black Hills from the south, she had frequently seen evidence of gold being worked, especially in the area around Custer City. But during the approach to Deadwood, Ellen soon recognized that the search for wealth was much more fiercely concentrated here. The beauty of the land was being stripped without mercy, the timbered ridges laid bare. In every ravine, rough-dressed men had pitched tents or erected makeshift pole shanties, while they roiled the streams with their pans or tore at the earth systematically, shovelful by shovelful, and sent it through the crude apparatus she had heard called "rockers." What the gold-hungry were doing to this country seemed a desecration to the apprentice actress.

The stage horses labored over a hump, and as they prepared to begin the long descent into Deadwood, Ellen peered from the window in disbelief: Deadwood swarmed! From wall to wall, the narrow, steep-sided valley was crowded with men and equipment, their dingy canvas tents clinging to any ground that was level enough to hold them. Along the heart of the gulch, Deadwood Creek, men labored over their placer claims, and rows of build-ings—some of canvas and rough-hewn lumber, some of log construction with shingle roofs and chimneys of stone and mud daubing—stood cheek-by-jowl flanking a narrow, twisting street. Others were perched on the hill behind that street or followed a second rudimentary street on the opposite side of the creek, which split this camp in two.

There were no sidewalks. Whether as a result of recent rains or an overflow from the creek, Main Street was a morass of mud. As the coach rolled through, the horses' hooves kicked it up, and anyone unfortunate enough to be on foot was unmercifully splattered with the same slop that sucked at his boots. A bull train, under dirt-streaked canvas, had halted in the center of the street, the oxen standing in the muck placidly unconcerned at the way they dammed up the flow of traffic. Piles of logs lay wherever they had been dumped.

As the stagecoach rolled farther into town, Ellen no-ticed that a tide of sound seemed to rise up to engulf it—from the open doors of saloons, from street corners where men had clustered to hear someone shouting about a mining claim he had for sale, or from a shell-game operator urging passersby to bet on their chances of out-guessing him and finding the elusive pea. Rough-looking men in drab clothing and the inevitable knee-high boots jostled each other as they poured in and out of the build-ings along the boggy pathway. The buildings housed a few businesses—a newspaper, hotels, general stores, and restaurants—but most by far were occupied by saloons, which seemed to do the greatest amount of trade. In front of one saloon, Ellen saw a man with a full dark beard who stood on a packing box, Bible in hand, exhorting the trickle of patrons to turn away from the evil influence of drink.

She glanced about at her fellow travelers, wondering if they shared her feelings of apprehension; mostly they seemed exhausted from the long stage ride. But one person, she discovered, did seem to know something of what was in her mind. Jack Langrishe, seated behind her, leaned forward to touch her shoulder. Turning her head, she caught the scent of brandy as he spoke.

"My dear, don't let your first look upset you. Remember, the rest of us have seen all this before—many times. These mining camps start out just about alike. They're wild enough at first, I grant you, but eventually they settle down."

Ellen smiled and looked back out the window as Langrishe continued. "Just remember that the people you see out there are human, after all. They may have come here out of greed, yet even so they have a right to some of the more civilizing influences of life, and we must help supply them. That's our job—it's the reason we're here." He added, "Ah! The Grand Central. Our hotel, I believe. . . ."

With a great amount of shouting—at his horses and at the bystanders, who swore as they were forced to scramble out of the way—the driver skillfully maneuvered his vehicle to the hotel entrance, close enough for his passengers to step directly onto the rough boards of the porch without getting into the mud.

Bruce Walker clambered out and then gave a hand to each of the women. The driver, having anchored his reins, was unloading baggage from the top of the coach, aided by Polk Renner—as much as he could help with his wounded arm. Costume trunks and boxes were handed down to the men of the company, while the women stood waiting and looking about uncertainly at this place that they would make their temporary home.

Jack Langrishe had disappeared into the hotel. He came back now, wearing a sober look, and called his actors to gather round. He seemed reluctant to tell his news. "They were expecting us," he said, "but there appears to be a shortage of space—not enough separate rooms for us all. So I'm sorry, but it looks as though I'll have to ask you to double up."

From his manner they had expected worse. "Not the first time for us," Bruce Walker said cheerfully. "We can put up with it. Whoever I get, I only hope he doesn't snore!"

Ellen caught a knowing wink and a smile from Bertie Clevenger, who stood nearby holding her little girl by the hand. The woman leaned closer to tell Ellen, in a whisper, "What most likely *really* happened was that Jack found out how much the rooms were going to cost. After moving everybody all this distance, he probably just couldn't afford it."

The group was breaking up. The leather shield over the rear boot had been unfastened, and members of the company crowded up to claim their belongings. Ellen Dorsey, hanging back, noticed that Claire Richards also was waiting, holding herself apart from the noisy proceedings. It had occurred to Ellen that she and this darkly handsome actress were the only two unattached women in the troupe, lacking either a husband or—as in the Clevenger widow's case—a child. But so far they had exchanged hardly a dozen words. To remedy this situation, Ellen walked across the rough planks of the porch and, with her warmest smile, said, "I hope you won't mind too much having me for a roommate, Miss Richards. Perhaps it won't be for more than a day or two."

The young woman turned her head. The dark eyes beneath her arched brows held such a look of disdain that Ellen was taken aback. Claire Richards said icily, "It won't be for even one day!"

Ellen found herself stammering. "But . . . but surely you heard what Mr. Langrishe told us just now . . . about having to share—"

"I mean to speak to Jack Langrishe," the other woman snapped. "I don't intend sharing a room with you or with anyone."

The sudden coldness in her cheeks told Ellen the blood had left them. Stung by hurt and humiliation, she could only stare as Claire Richards walked away from her.

But then she felt an arm slip around her waist, and Bertie Clevenger was there, speaking reassuring words. "You mustn't let her upset you. It doesn't matter in the least. You can move in with us."

Ellen turned and saw the older woman's friendly smile. She looked at her and at the little girl. "I'd love to. But—you've got Cindy. It would be much too crowded."

"Nonsense! Probably we can have a cot moved in. I

don't want to hear any more about it. I've already claimed your suitcase for you. Now, you come along with us. . . ."

The room was tiny and sparingly furnished with a brass bed, a commode, and a couple of straight-backed chairs. A curtained-off corner concealed a wooden pole fastened diagonally between the walls to serve for a closet. The rough lumber of the floor had already begun to buckle, and the window's casing had warped, so that Ellen had to work to raise the sash and let fresh air into the place.

Cindy Clevenger, a pretty, quiet child of eight with long blond curls and a face that was a miniature of her mother's, sat on the bed crooning to the ragged doll cradled in her arms. Bertie was taking garments from her bag to hang in the makeshift closet as she chatted in friendly fashion about the acting company Ellen now belonged to.

"The theater can be a hard life sometimes, honey, and unfortunately actors aren't always the most practical people you could meet. I've been with Jack Langrishe for half a dozen years, and I've never known him when he wasn't struggling just to get by and pay our wages. Every new strike—every mining camp where we've played—he's always had the hope that he'd somehow manage to get hold of a claim that would make his fortune. It has never worked out yet, but he's always followed his rainbow . . . and now it's led him here. Chances are he'll only be disappointed again."

She added quickly, "Not that I'm criticizing, you understand. Jack's a good and generous man and a real artist. But . . . practical?" As though aware suddenly that she was doing all the talking, she turned from her work to find the younger woman standing at the window, gazing down into the street without really seeing it. Frowning, the widow crossed the room. "Ellen? Are you all right, dear?"

Ellen Dorsey nodded, but she could not hide the tears that blurred her eyes. Understanding the problem, Bertie placed a soothing hand on her shoulder. "I hope you're not still letting yourself fret over our leading lady."

Ellen flung out her hands. "But, Mrs. Clevenger—"

"That's Bertie," the other woman firmly corrected her.

This resulted in a smile and a nod. "Thank you, Bertie. And thank you for being so good to me. I'm sure you understand how it feels to be the new member of a company when the others already know each other and have worked together. I want so much for you all to like me and accept me—not resent me for being an intruder!"

"You are not intruding!" the older woman emphatically assured her. "Get that idea out of your head. *We're* lucky Jack was able to find someone like you, on such short notice—we'd be in real trouble about now without an ingenue. But also, you mustn't judge us all by Claire Richards's behavior out there. What you've been seeing really isn't like her. Try to remember that she has her own problems—the main one being that she's a jealous woman."

Ellen could only stare, incredulous. "Surely not jealous of *me*? That's just ridiculous. Why—she's beautiful!"

Bertie Clevenger gave a sniff. "Well, as far as that's concerned, don't go putting *yourself* down. What's more, you're younger than Claire, and you have a freshness she must know she's beginning to lose. On top of which, she's very much aware of being the star of this company. Has it occurred to you that she might have it in her head that you've joined up with the idea of trying to push her aside?"

"Oh, I'd never *dream*—" Ellen cried, aghast. "Bertie, I swear, I never—"

"Honey, you don't have to—not to me. I never suspected any such thing, not for a minute. I'm only trying to guess what might be in *her* head—not yours, or mine either." Having said that, the woman hesitated, frowning, as though reluctant to say what came next.

"I guess you had better know," she went on gruffly, "there's another reason for Claire's nose to be out of joint. After all, you did sit next to him in the coach, all the way up from Cheyenne." She nodded at the stunned look that was forming on Ellen's face. "Oh, yes, our star is pretty far gone on Mr. Bruce Walker and has been for some time now. Everybody in the company knows it. Up to now she's had him to herself, and the rest of us thought he was pretty serious about *her*—anyway, as serious as it was possible for a fellow like that to be about anything. Yet from the moment you stepped into the stagecoach that morning, it was almost as though he thought Claire Richards had ceased to exist."

Ellen was shaking her head in shock and bewilderment. "I had no way at all of knowing this. . . ."

"Naturally not—how could you? And I do have to admit that Bruce Walker is a very engaging young fellow, especially when he makes up his mind to it. You *were* attracted, weren't you?"

She had to admit it and felt her cheeks grow warm. "But believe me, the last thing I'd have wanted was to be the cause of trouble."

A motherly arm went around Ellen and squeezed her. "Just don't let yourself worry too much about it. The way you pitched in to help back at that stage stop—*that* told me a lot about what kind of a person you are. You and I are going to be good friends."

"Oh, I know we are!" Impulsively, Ellen kissed her on the cheek.

Disturbing as she found many of the things the Clevenger woman had told her, she was grateful, too. At least there was one person here in this raw new country who liked her well enough to want to talk seriously to her and to help ease a difficult adjustment.

But then she thought, *No—not just one*. For all at once she was remembering Tom Murdock—that blunt and direct man who had talked with her so earnestly and interestedly for so long back at Anderson's station. How odd that she would think of him at this moment, recalling his sober manner and his not-too-handsome features, which contrasted so sharply with Bruce Walker's blond good looks and easy, bantering charm.

Odder still that two men so utterly dissimilar could each have made so strong and favorable an impression. . . .

Chapter 4

Having cleaned up, put on fresh linen, and carefully brushed his clothing and polished his boots, Jack Langrishe was ready. He donned a bowler at precisely the angle he liked and, thus prepared, stepped out of the Grand Central Hotel for his first appraising look at this camp, where for better or worse he had chosen to cast his lot.

Shafts of golden light bordered by deep shadows lay over the camp in the slow waning of the summer afternoon, casting a softening patina on the ragged tents and rough buildings. From long acquaintance with such places, Langrishe was able to look beneath the rawness of Deadwood to the town that might someday be. Already he noticed frame buildings going up to replace the first shoddy tents and thrown-together log shanties. With luck these, too, would one day give way—to solid brick structures. The bottomless mud of Main Street would eventually be paved over and bordered with sidewalks. He knew well enough that all this was possible, because he had seen it happen elsewhere. On the other hand, this Deadwood could die as quickly as it had been born, to become just another in a litany of decayed and forgotten ghost towns. Time alone would tell.

Peering across the busy street, he spotted something that interested him, and he halted for a thoughtful look at a fair-sized building lot lying vacant in the very heart of camp—the perfect spot, he thought judiciously, for his theater. Nothing pretentious to begin with, of course. A wooden frame to enclose the auditorium; a canvas roof to keep out the rain. Poor enough, but all he could likely afford at the outset.

"After all," Jack Langrishe murmured aloud, as was his habit when thinking things through, "the Globe itself hardly amounted to more. And if it was good enough for Shakespeare . . ."

With plans, expenses, and estimates humming in his head, he turned away. Gold Street entered Main at that point, and Langrishe gingerly picked his way across the soupy intersection and turned up the side street. At the hotel, he had inquired as to whether the camp boasted a newspaper, and now the clapboard building with the painted sign of the Pioneer Printing Office came clearly into view.

Entering, he was met by the aromas of machine oil, paper, and printer's ink—they never failed to stimulate him. In fact, Jack Langrishe actually thought sometimes he should have chosen journalism for his profession rather than the stage. A lanky fellow who was doing something to a small flatbed press looked up from his work long enough to say curtly, "Boss isn't here."

"Very well. I'll drop back later. In the meantime"—Langrishe took out a folded sheet of paper covered with his neat handwriting—"would you please see that he gets this? It's an announcement that should be of interest to his readers. I have it all written out—he can run it just as it stands."

The man wiped oil from his hands with a rag and took the paper. He glanced it over without any show of interest. "All right."

Well, some people were just too dull to appreciate the excitement and glamour of the theater, Langrishe was thinking. But then he shrugged and said, "Tell your employer I'll be having some work for him—posters, handbills, tickets, programs . . ."

"All right."

There were questions he had intended to ask, but Langrishe doubted the value of any answers he would get from this gent. Instead, he said good day and left, hanging back long enough to see his document carelessly impaled on a spike amid the litter of a poker table that obviously served as the editor's desk. He supposed he had achieved as much as he could hope for.

Returning to Main Street, he thought a moment of crossing to get a better look at that vacant lot. But then he considered the deep sea of mire that lay between, and looking at his trousers and neatly polished boots, he said aloud, "Not just now . . ." Then he resumed his course along the north side of the street, which twisted and slanted its way down the throat of the gulch; and he threaded his way through the jostling crowds of jackbooted miners, bullwhackers, drifters, and others who swarmed through this camp and tramped in and out of its wide-open doorways. As he did, he noted with interest the painted signs identifying various businesses—a drug store, a dentist, a barbershop, a meat market and grocery. . . . It was remarkable how many essential services had already taken root in a community that was something under six months old.

With it all, one had the impression that nearly every other establishment was a saloon or gambling hall. Through their doors the strong smell of raw liquor reached out temptingly to Jack Langrishe; mixed with it was the boisterous talk of the men who lined the plank bars and the arguments of the men at the gaming tables. Passing one such place, he heard curses, then a thud of fists and the trampling of boots as a fight began and men hastened to clear out of the way. Langrishe didn't pause to find out what it was about.

He wanted to see the whole length of the street, and so he walked on, turning back only when he reached a point near the bottom of the gulch where another artery, Sherman Street, after roughly paralleling Main, joined it in a crude V.

Beyond this point, the look of the town was different, and so were the silent and impassive faces. "Hong Kee, Washing & Ironing"—as he read the words and saw other names like it, a vagrant drift of incense caught his attention; he nodded with understanding. Many camps like Deadwood had a Chinatown almost from the first day they sprouted into life. On completion of the transcontinental railroad, the coolie labor imported to build it had to have places to go. The mining frontier had offered desirable employment for them as cooks or laundrymen, but it also subjected them to the most menial chores, chores that white men found to be beneath them.

Turning back up the street, Langrishe noticed a row of grubby shacks and recognized them for the only thing they could be—cribs for prostitution. After he passed the Bella Union Dance Hall, he paused before a building next to it with a sign that read "Saloon No. 10, Carl Mann and Wm. Nuttall, Props." Head to one side, he murmured, "Are there so many saloons in this camp that they give them numbers instead of names?" It looked a quieter place than some others farther up in the heart of the camp. He fingered the coins in his pocket, considered his thirst, and on an impulse he entered.

It was a small establishment, with room for only a plain wooden bar, a few gaming tables, and stools for the players. Four men were engaged in a desultory hand of poker, while another sat nearby with his stool tilted back against the wall and his hands empty in his lap, watching listlessly. No one was behind the bar as Langrishe came in, but a dumpy, bald-headed fellow laid down his cards and called out, "Can I help you?"

"You may indeed, landlord," Langrishe assured him in a voice that filled the room. Having counted the house and done some quick computing of his resources, he tossed a couple of silver coins on the wood and ordered, "Drinks all around, if you please."

"Coming up." The little man rose and hurried around to set out the glasses and fill them. The others were already heading for the bar.

Taking his glass, lifting it in a general salute, Langrishe tossed off his drink. Afterward, he announced, "The name, gentlemen, is John S. Langrishe—Jack, to my friends. And I trust we are all friends here?"

The bald-headed man reached across the counter to shake hands. "I'm Carl Mann. My partner, Billy Nuttall, ain't in at the moment." He introduced the others. The three poker players were all prospectors. One of them, though, an old fellow named Bill Massie, wore graying side-whiskers and a billed cap, from which Langrishe gathered that he was, in fact, a retired Mississippi steamboat captain.

The fifth person, a man in his mid-twenties who had been seated alone watching the game, had something about him that bothered Langrishe. It might have been nothing more than a nervous manner and the fact that his nose had been broken and one of his eyes was slightly crossed—certainly nothing to be held against a man. But as an actor Jack Langrishe considered himself a good observer and judge of character, and he at once put this man, Jack McCall, down as something of a ne'er-do-well— and not to be trusted.

Mann, the saloon owner, now offered Langrishe a drink on the house, and after accepting, the actor genially said, "But that makes my limit." Afterward he laid his hat on the bar and ran a hand across his bald scalp. He was trying not to feel depressed over the fact that no one had responded to his name or seemed to realize who he was.

Suddenly one of the group exclaimed, "Hold on! I know about you. . . . You must be the actor!"

"That is correct," he answered, his spirits quickly lifting.

"I heard you was coming to Deadwood," the man went on, then spoiled it all by adding, "Somebody at the hotel said some actor with that name had written 'em for rooms. . . ."

Thinking *Better than nothing*, Langrishe decided to make the most of it. "My company arrived just this afternoon—twenty talented artists." In actuality there were a few more than half that number, but he didn't consider himself to be under oath. "We shall soon be offering this camp a repertoire of drama—comedy as well as tragedy—and other entertainment to suit each and every taste. All we lack at the moment is a theater. However, I was noticing a property that should be the ideal location for one: two blocks up, on the south side of Main, opposite the mouth of Gold Street. Does anyone present know if it's been spoken for?"

"Kind of hard to say," Mann told him. "Nearly every square foot of the gulch is claimed by somebody or other, but as far as town lots are concerned . . . well, this is still an Indian reservation. Nobody but the Sioux can legally own any part of it."

Captain Massie suggested, "Quickest way to learn where you stand would be just to start building. If somebody figures he has a better claim, you can bet you'll hear from him!"

Langrishe shook his head. "That's hardly my style. If there's any dispute, I'd prefer to settle it first in a friendly manner if possible. But meanwhile my people can't just sit around. They're anxious to set up someplace and start rehearsals." He could have added, *And try to get some money into the coffers.* "So it appears I may have a problem."

Carl Mann said, "You want a theater? The Bella Union might be available—right next door."

Langrishe remembered seeing the place. "It looked to me like a dance hall."

"That's what it is. But at least it's got a stage, and there's a curtain, footlights—everything. Tom Miller has his girls put on acts when they ain't hustling, and on occasion Tom gets up himself and plays the bones. The place ain't much for class, but he might be willing to rent it to you, reasonable, while you see about arranging for something permanent. All you have to do is take out the tables and put in some seats and you're ready for business."

The notion did begin to sound intriguing as Jack Langrishe considered it. Cheerfully, he admitted, "I've performed under worse conditions. . . . I may talk to your Mr. Tom Miller—and meanwhile, thank you, friend, for the suggestion." He picked up his hat. "For now, I'll bid you all good evening."

He left with their good wishes in his ears and a more optimistic feeling about this camp and the people in it. "Not at all a bad sort," he told himself, and then added, "All but one . . ." He was thinking of the cross-eyed Jack McCall, who could safely be put down as a ruffian . . . but perhaps not so easily dismissed. There had been something in the way the fellow had watched him leave that reminded him of how a cat might size up a prospective mouse. . . .

Langrishe had spent longer than he thought in the No. 10. The sun had dropped behind the western horizon, and dusk was already seeping into the gulch, with lamps now burning all up and down the length of Main Street. The place was starting to liven up as miners with a hard day of work behind them and gold dust in their pouches began to pour into camp from their claims. The Bella Union, however, remained dark, its door closed and padlocked. "Well, another time perhaps," Langrishe murmured, and he started up the street again.

Retracing his steps past the No. 10, he saw someone silhouetted against the doorway, watching him pass. The lean shape of Jack McCall came instantly to his mind, and it was as though a warning bell sounded faintly. Passing on from a patch of light into shadow and out again, he remained constantly aware of the sinister figure behind him. When he came to the recess of a darkened doorway, he sidestepped into it and from a pocket of his coat took a little two-shot derringer. Knowing about the dangers of the place he was headed for, he had bought it as a precaution just before leaving Denver.

In the shadows he waited, ignoring the sporadic flow of foot traffic past his doorway, watching for one particular shape. Suddenly he clamped down on his breathing. The figure of McCall appeared, lined against the garishly lighted facade of a saloon across the street, close enough to the doorway for him to have touched Langrishe. As though puzzled at having lost his quarry, McCall came to a halt. He pivoted slowly where he stood, throwing a glance along the street, and as he did, a gleam of lamplight caught the muzzle of a pistol in his hand.

Jack Langrishe didn't give himself time to think. Face grim, he grabbed McCall's wrist with his left hand and jerked him around, at the same moment shoving the barrel of the derringer into the fellow's ribs. McCall's breath left him in a gasp, and he froze.

"Were you looking for me?" Langrishe demanded. Getting no answer, he added, "I'll take that." There was no resistance when he snatched the pistol from McCall's fingers. Holding both weapons, he said through clenched teeth, "I just don't care for being followed."

With the derringer removed from his belly, McCall got control of his tongue. "I—I wasn't following you. . . ."

"I don't care for liars, either!" Langrishe snapped.

Langrishe found he was trembling slightly—from anger and from the risk he had just taken. He was in no sense a man of violence, but as a trained actor, he was determined not to let this man know that. Summoning up his deepest, most foreboding stage voice, he spoke a chill warning: "Villain! I have no doubt that seeing someone decently dressed, with money at hand to buy drinks for strangers, you took me for fair game. Unluckily for you, I surmised what you had in mind. I assure you that I never forget a face. It will behoove you to keep yours out of my sight, as long as we both remain in this community! You understand me, sir?"

The man only glowered; he had learned that here was one tenderfoot who had proved somewhat tougher than he looked. For his part, Langrishe was ready to believe that this Jack McCall, though he might not look like much, was capable of almost any mischief. Now, getting no argument, he gave the scoundrel's gun a toss that sent it spinning into the middle of the street. McCall gave a hoarse cry as he saw it sink into the mire, where he would have no easy time finding it again.

"For now," Langrishe said, rounding off the scene with a suitable exit line, "I leave you to contemplate your sins. I have no doubt they are legion. Good evening to you, sir!" And with that he turned his back on Jack McCall's dumbfounded gaze and walked away up the street, toward the Grand Central Hotel.

Chapter 5

It was at the tail end of another July day, full of hot sun and scudding clouds, that Tom Murdock and Art Willard, one of his guards, came dragging into Deadwood on horseback. A few hours earlier, the southbound stage, which Willard had been escorting to Custer City with its shipment of gold dust, had been attacked—and this time its valuable cargo had been stolen, though no one on board had been injured. As soon as the stage reached nearby Custer City, Willard found Murdock, who was stationed at the stage office, and they set off together on the trail of the bandits.

The search had proved fruitless. Now, with the dust and fatigue of a long ride on them, Murdock and the guard made directly for the headquarters of the stage line in Deadwood, on Sherman Street at the edge of town, to break the news to George Faraday.

The office was in a frame building with a barn and corral adjoining, and with one of the company's Concord stagecoaches, already well battered by use before the partnership acquired it, parked in the side yard. They drew rein, and Art Willard, a stolid and no-nonsense fellow, looked at his chief and said, "Sorry I couldn't stop the holdup, Tom."

"Nothing for you to apologize for," Murdock told him. "You gave it your best, short of getting yourself killed—and I don't ask my men to do that. Better luck next time. Go get some rest and a meal under your belt. It's what we both need."

Willard lifted a hand in salute and rode on. Murdock wearily swung down from the saddle. He anchored his horse to a tie ring beside the door and went up the two plank steps and inside, batting dust from his hat against a knee.

Murdock's partner, George Faraday, was seated at the desk talking to his yard manager, and they both turned around quickly. They must have read Murdock's expression; Faraday gave a sigh and a shake of his gaunt, silver-maned head and asked, "What happened?"

"I'm afraid today's shipment is lost," Murdock acknowledged. He nodded to the yard manager, Sid Krauss, and, perching himself on a corner of the desk, went on tiredly to explain. "They attacked just this side of Custer. Nobody was hurt, but they got the dust. The coach wasn't damaged, and it went on to Custer." Murdock sighed loudly, rubbing the grit from his eyes. "Art and I went after them. There was a trail of sorts to begin with—three riders—but they soon split up, and we lost them in some surface rock, over beyond the Whitewood. We never managed to pick them up again."

Faraday was a gentle-natured man, whom Murdock had never known to swear. He ran a palm down over the folds of his cheeks, and the droop of his shoulders showed how this latest news had hit him. He suggested, "Do you suppose—if you'd managed to get on the trail sooner—"

"It wouldn't have made that much difference. They knew what they were doing. Anyway, Art Willard and I set off on the trail just as soon as he reached Custer. There's no sense in blaming anyone."

"I wasn't intending to. It's just that—well, this came in yesterday." He indicated a letter on the desk in front of him.

"From Mel?" Murdock meant Mel Jenson, the third partner in this stage-line venture.

George Faraday nodded. "It's just like all the others. Every shipment we lose makes it that much harder for Mel to do a selling job for us. And we need every dime of business and credit he can raise."

Murdock said bleakly, "I know, George. But, I don't see what there is to do but keep going."

"I never considered doing anything else. . . . You

look beat, Tom," the senior partner added with a look of real concern. "You go take care of yourself. We'll discuss this later."

"Some grub is what I need mostly." Sliding off the corner of the desk, Murdock looked at the yard manager. "Sid, I left my horse tied out front. Would you see that someone gives him a rubdown and a good graining?"

Sid Krauss, a man of forty, had thinning yellow hair and blue eyes in a weathered, broad-cheeked face. He was a good worker, but one who always seemed overwrought, with some inner problem eating at him. He said, "Sure thing, Tom."

Murdock left the office. At a bench near the stable entrance he stripped off his gun belt and shirt, filled a wash basin from a bucket of creek water, and was sluicing dust and sweat from his face and body when Polk Renner found him. "How's the arm?" Murdock wanted to know.

"Oh, hell, it's all right." Renner flexed it, for proof. "I told you all along, I wasn't really hurt."

"You ought to give credit where it's due. Seems to me you got the widow, Mrs. Clevenger, to thank. And speaking of the widow,"—he went on before Renner could give him an argument—"how are those theater people that I met at Anderson's getting along? Are they all set up?"

"I reckon," Polk Renner said gruffly, as though mention of Mrs. Clevenger was somehow embarrassing. "They've taken over the Bella Union. Coming right along with rehearsals—or so I understand." He quickly changed to a safer subject. "I hear you been chasing stickups. No luck, I take it."

"Nope." Toweling off with a burlap sack, Murdock repeated the story of failure. "Like I told George, we're dealing with real professionals. What about that last run you took to Custer City?"

"Smooth as silk—no trouble at all." With a look of disgust Renner added, "Wouldn't you know it would be like that—no trouble when we didn't happen to be carrying any dust. Professionals, hah! I'm beginning to think what we're dealing with is mind readers."

Troubled, he watched in silence while his boss pulled a clean shirt over his head and shoved the tails inside his trousers. "And just how the hell are you, anyway, Tom?" Polk Renner blurted. "I swear, I dunno how you keep up this pace. It's the first time in a week that you've lit long enough for a man to get in a word with you . . . or give you some news—something I think you might find interesting. . . ."

Murdock stopped combing his wet hair with his fingers and said, "You have news?"

Renner nodded his head. "It could just be. . . . I been putting out the word, quiet-like, that I'd be interested in learning what I could about a man with a scar on his face. You know who I mean." He moved a finger slantwise across his forehead, across one eye to the cheek below it.

"And?"

"I now have a report on him from two different sources. Looks like his name is Bart Ryan—and he's been seen hanging out, big as life, at Johnny Varnes's place."

"Varnes!" Murdock echoed. His eyes narrowed.

"Surprised?"

"I'm not sure. From what I know of him, I guess nothing could surprise me too much. Have you checked into this?"

"I was about ready to when I heard you was back in camp. I thought you might want to deal with it personally."

"You thought right. This could just be the nearest thing to a break that we've had. Johnny Varnes, eh?" Murdock repeated the name, and there was a hard gleam in his eye. He strapped on his gun belt and picked up his hat from the bench. "No point in putting it off. Why don't the two of us go pay him a little visit . . . right now."

Johnny Varnes operated the biggest gambling hall in the gulch. It was simple in design: a large canvas roof stretched above bare wooden walls, its front wide open to Main Street, its floor merely the leveled ground spread with sawdust. Though his establishment was crude, Varnes's enterprise was a major achievement, for all the equipment that was crammed into the place—the card tables and faro layouts, the dice and roulette tables, and the big wheel of fortune, to say nothing of the ornate cherrywood bar that stretched along one entire wall—had been freighted in by bull team over roads that were primitive at best.

The hall would have been large enough for a town like Cheyenne or Denver, but here in Deadwood the pace of its business hardly subsided from one sunup to the next. Day or night, Johnny Varnes's bartenders and card dealers had their hands full. His lookouts, seated on high stools that gave a clear view of the activity, were always on the alert, with shotguns across their knees.

Tom Murdock was not a gambling man—nor much of a drinking one for that matter—and with the press of stage-line business keeping him constantly on the road, he had done little more than glance into Varnes's place in passing. Now he and Polk Renner walked in and made their way through the crowd that half filled the tent, a crowd that would grow larger and louder as evening came on. They searched the bar and tables, studying faces, but finally had to conclude that the man they were looking for wasn't there.

They gave it up and worked their way to the bar, where they tried a shot of the local whiskey and found it no better or worse than expected. Leaning against the bar, Polk Renner looked over the action and muttered sourly, "How many *honest* games you reckon get played here?"

"One thing's sure," Murdock said, "a man could go broke finding out."

"Well, if you was to ask me—" Renner broke off, and gave his boss a quick warning nudge with an elbow. "Watch it!"

Two men had entered through a door in a partition at the rear of the tent and were moving toward the bar. Murdock watched them approach. He had seen Johnny Varnes only a few times before, but enough to recognize him now: a tall and remarkably lean fellow, almost gaunt, with jet black hair and brows. His lean cheeks had been pitted by some past illness, and his prominent jaw made him look swarthy, with a heavy stubble that no razor could touch. His eyes were black and piercing as they fixed on Tom Murdock.

At Varnes's elbow was Creed Dunning, not as tall as his boss but perhaps thirty pounds heavier—a solid slab of a man, with a cap of reddish hair lying close to his round and battered skull. Dunning looked like a prizefighter, and rumor had it that he at one time had been one. Now Varnes's chief bouncer and right-hand man, he seemed satisfied to rely less on his battle-scarred fists than on the big, wooden-handled six-shooter he wore in a holster against one heavy thigh.

The two men walked along the bar directly toward Murdock and halted, Johnny Varnes with fists on hips, the skirts of his coat flung back to reveal a checkered vest and, stretching across it, a watch chain made of gold nuggets. "Here is a surprise!" he said, with a smile that didn't seem quite genuine. "You're Murdock, aren't you? I never expected to be seeing you in my place. Busy fellow like you—getting rich running that stage line—I took it for granted you never had time to waste on frivolous things like normal human beings."

Tom Murdock made no attempt to match his manner. "We're not here to play games with anybody," he said shortly. "We were told this was the place we might find somebody we're looking for—a man with a knife scar on his face."

"Oh?" Varnes made a gesture with one hand. "Go ahead—look around. You should find at least a dozen like that. Hereabouts, a good many differences get settled at knife point."

"We'd have no trouble picking him out," Murdock said, "even though the last time we saw him the lower half of his face was covered. It couldn't hide that scar." He demonstrated, running a thumbnail down across his own brow and cheek. He added, "We want to find him because he's been involved in at least three holdup attempts on our stages. Oh, yes—we've even got a name for him: Bart Ryan."

No one would have thought, from Varnes's immobile features, that the description or the name meant anything to him. To the man at his elbow, he said, "Creed, do we know anybody like that?"

Creed Dunning shrugged his meaty shoulders. "A lot of drifters through the gulch are in and out of this tent. Man can't keep track of 'em all."

Polk Renner, who had been silent up to this point, said blandly, "Funny . . . seems like someone told me about seeing you and Ryan together, Dunning. More'n a couple of times."

The big man's stare settled on Renner. "Who the hell told you a thing like that?"

"Never mind who. What they said, the pair of you was thick as thieves—if you'll excuse the expression," Renner added with an evil smirk.

Creed Dunning stiffened, and his face grew dark with anger. But Johnny Varnes showed no emotion as he told Murdock, "I'd say you've been paying too much heed to rumors. As for this so-called stage robber, this Bart Ryan . . . well, I guarantee you won't find him here. But be my guest! Go right ahead and look. And then . . . get out!"

Polk Renner gave a snort. "Almost sounds like somebody tipped you off we was comin', maybe?"

That got him a look from Varnes and a quiet admonition from Murdock. "All right, Polk."

To the gambler, Murdock said, "We've already done our looking, Varnes. We didn't see him." He glanced toward the door in the rear partition of the gambling hall. "What's back there?"

"A private office," Creed answered him loudly. "And you'll stay the hell out!"

"No, no," Varnes corrected his man hastily. "I don't mind. Help yourself, Murdock, if it'll make you happier."

But the stage-line owner shook his head. "You're too willing. That means he won't be there either. Well, maybe another time."

"Oh, no, Murdock!" Johnny Varnes's tone halted him as he started to leave. He spoke quietly, but there was an edge of iron in his voice. "No other time, ever! You've come here with insinuations and not a shred of evidence.

If you come again, you'd better bring the proof—and perhaps a few more guns wouldn't hurt."

Tom Murdock's level stare accepted the thinly veiled challenge. "You can count on it!" he said curtly. "If we have to come again, we'll bring whatever's needed." Then he gave a summoning nod to Polk Renner and turned on his heel toward the door.

The other two men watched them go, and then Creed Dunning turned to his employer and saw the cold gleam that had come into his hard, black eyes. When Johnny Varnes spoke, in a voice too quiet to reach other ears than their own, Dunning sensed the savage anger behind the words.

"I hope you're satisfied! I told you to do something to throw Murdock off the scent. Instead you've given the whole game away—and you let him walk in here and make a fool of me!"

There was no other man Dunning would have allowed to speak to him in that tone. Even so, he was roused to anger. "That ain't fair! How was I to know he had Bart Ryan spotted? And what's the difference—he can't prove nothing."

"That's beside the point!" snapped Varnes. "Don't go underestimating Tom Murdock. He talks quiet, but he's smart. And sometimes the quiet kind can be the most dangerous." He added, "In any event, you'll have to get rid of Bart Ryan. Now that Murdock knows him, he's less than no good to me."

"Dammit, Johnny! Bart's one of the best men we've got! I'll give you my guarantee—next time I use him, I'll make sure there's no way to see that scar."

Varnes considered that a long moment, his cold stare resting on Creed Dunning in a way that made the man squirm. "You'd better!" Varnes said finally. "Just remember this: I've got big plans for this camp. I don't intend for anyone to spoil them. Not Tom Murdock, and certainly not some hired gunman who can't follow orders without messing up. You understand me?"

"Sure, Johnny."

Without another word, Varnes turned and stalked off

toward his office at the rear of the tent. As soon as he was gone, Dunning signaled for one of the bartenders to fill a glass for him.

Ruthless, and totally confident in the revolver that filled his belt holster, Creed Dunning hated to admit fear of any man. But after that tongue-lashing from Johnny Varnes, he discovered that he was sweating. Moreover, there was a faint tremor in his hand as he took up the drink.

Chapter 6

Outside the gambling tent, away from the traffic heading toward its open front, Polk Renner was still fuming as he and Tom Murdock walked off. "What the hell do you make of that? Is Varnes just touchy at so many questions—or was he really covering for Bart Ryan? Seems to me he didn't give all that much of a damn whether we believed him or not."

"I know," Tom Murdock conceded. "Almost seems like it didn't matter to him if we stumbled onto the idea that *all* our trouble is coming from that private office of his."

The older man looked at him sharply. "You reckon, maybe? Somehow I never even thought of him in that connection—just took him for a tinhorn with a tad more enterprise than most. Still, we've both been wondering if somebody here in Deadwood—somebody with a brain—mightn't be behind the campaign against our stages. . . . Would he fill the bill?"

Murdock didn't answer at once. His frown was thoughtful as they turned to walk along the busy center of Deadwood. He said finally, "Johnny Varnes always struck me as somebody to be taken seriously. He's smart enough that he could turn his hand to almost anything—and it strikes me Creed Dunning isn't one who would hesitate to carry out almost any kind of order. They'll both bear watching." Then he added, with an abrupt change of subject, "The next thing on my mind is catching up with a couple of meals I seem to have missed!"

Renner had an immediate suggestion. "I could use a bite, myself. Hey, why don't we step across to the Grand

Central? I've taken to eating there lately. They got some new help in the kitchen that turns out the best meals in camp."

Murdock held back. "I wasn't rightly thinking about a hotel dining room." He ran a palm across a two-day growth of whiskers. "I'd be a little out of place."

"In Deadwood?" Polk Renner scoffed. "Hmmph! You ain't serious. Now come along. . . ."

Reluctantly, Tom Murdock let himself be herded toward the big frame building halfway down the gulch. The rains had ended just days ago, but already steady traffic had beaten the street mud to ankle-deep powder. They waded through this, dodging a flatbed wagon loaded with lumber from one of the steam sawmills that were rapidly denuding the nearby ridges of their timber. As they stepped up onto the porch of the hotel, Murdock turned back for a second look at a man who was moving on down the steep slant of the street. He caught at his companion's elbow. "Wait up! Would that be who I thought it was?"

Polk Renner followed his glance and nodded. "Yeah, that was who you thought. That was Hickok—Wild Bill himself!"

Murdock was still staring after the gunfighter, a subject of legends. Somebody just now had halted the man for a word with him. As Hickok listened patiently, Murdock was able to get a good look at him—a real giant of a man, well built and carrying himself erect. Though the last light of evening was beginning to fade, there was no mistaking the tawny mane falling onto the broad shoulders, the hawkish features that were clean shaven except for the horns of a full and drooping mustache. Hickok was meticulously dressed, in a Prince Albert coat and flat-brimmed hat. Murdock thought he glimpsed a long-barreled revolver strapped high against one leg.

To his friend, Murdock said, "What in the world would he be doing in Deadwood?"

Polk Renner shrugged. "What's any of us doing here? Planning to get rich—what else? He come in day before yesterday from Cheyenne, riding with a wagon train put together by his friends Steve and Colorado Charlie Utter.

I hear the three of 'em are sharing a tent, and the Utter boys are talking about setting up a pony mail express to operate twixt here and the railroad."

"And Hickok?"

"I ain't too sure what *he's* got in mind. As it happens, I found a chance this morning to stand him a drink and jaw with him a few minutes—I always been curious to meet up with the West's most famous shootist. And I must say, he surprised me. I found him a mild-spoken sort . . . and perfectly willing to answer my questions. Did you know, he's married?"

"Since when?"

"This spring, I understand, to a woman who owns a circus. Hadn't been for that, Bill told me, he'd probably have gone scouting again for George Custer—which means he'd more'n likely have been one of them that lost their hair at the Little Big Horn last month. But Wild Bill, he went on a honeymoon instead. Now his wife is back in Cincinnati, and he's here looking for a stake."

"Prospecting?"

"So he says. But it looks like he's doing it mostly over a poker table in Carl Mann's saloon. I just don't think he has it in him to do much good swinging a pick or a shovel. Tom, you'd swear he's an old man. Truth is, he's younger'n me—not even forty, they say—but seeing him close up, Hickok strikes me as just about burnt out, with something in the look of his eyes like he doesn't even *see* you when you're talking to him."

Downstreet from them, the tall man had finished his conversation and was moving on, unhurriedly, in and out of the shadows. Awed, Tom Murdock watched him go—this man, reputed to be the finest marksman ever known, with rifle *or* handgun, had been not only a famous army scout during and after the Civil War, but also the town tamer at Hays City and the wide-open cattle mart of Abilene, Kansas.

At Murdock's elbow, Polk Renner continued. "Charlie Utter told me that in the past few days he's heard Bill say more'n once he pretty much expects to die here in the Black Hills. Can you imagine Wild Bill Hickok talking like that?" And when Murdock had no answer, Renner said abruptly, "Well, let's go. I'm getting hungrier by the minute!"

They had no more than entered the hotel dining room when Murdock understood why his friend had made such a point of eating there. The first persons he saw were the woman who had doctored Polk's arm, Bertie Clevenger, and her little girl, Cindy, seated at one of the tables. As soon as Polk Renner appeared, the beguiling blond girl gave him a big grin and an eager wave, and her mother smiled and nodded in greeting. Murdock commented dryly, "You seem to be real popular with the Clevenger family."

His friend had turned slightly red of face. "We get along all right. Bertie, now—she's a real fine woman. Lost her husband to the fever a few years back. Naturally, I've wanted to do anything I could to help her and the kid feel at home in Deadwood."

"Naturally."

Renner caught him by the sleeve. "Come on. They'll be wanting us to sit with them."

Murdock wanted to back out, but the other man dragged him forward. A change had come over Polk Renner in the past few minutes: The man who had just now stood up to Varnes and Dunning, trading threats without batting an eye, seemed suddenly ill at ease and in need of reassurance. He had pulled off his hat, and as he approached the table, he held the hat firmly in both hands. He could only swallow without answering when Bertie Clevenger said, "How nice to see you Mr. Renner. And Mr. Murdock . . ."

Tom Murdock managed a greeting, but when she asked them to sit, Renner could only say meekly—as if to a schoolmarm—"Yes, ma'am." He slid onto a chair. "Thank you, ma'am. . . ."

Tom Murdock hesitated, and as he did, he heard his name called. Looking up, he saw Ellen Dorsey at another table with a good-looking man, whom he recognized as being another of the Langrishe company. She smiled, beckoning. Murdock excused himself and walked over to her, feeling suddenly more out of place than ever.

Ellen looked clean and fresh—and as pretty as he remembered. She sounded quite sincere as she told him, "It's nice to see you again. You remember Bruce Walker. . . ."

"I remember seeing him that day at Anderson's." He shook the hand the actor reached to him. Walker's hand was smooth, uncallused; his answering smile was cool and self-assured.

Murdock hesitated when Ellen said, "We haven't ordered yet. Won't you join us?"

"I wouldn't want to butt in."

"Not at all," the other man assured him. Walker's manner was civil enough, even if lacking in enthusiasm. There seemed no way to get out of the situation. Murdock, unshaven and aware of how he contrasted with Walker's well-groomed appearance, thought, *Damn that Polk Renner!* But he gingerly took a seat and dropped his dusty hat to the floor beside his boot.

A waiter came for their orders. Afterward, Bruce Walker, who had been eyeing the other man, said, "I understand you're a partner in a stage line, Murdock."

"When I first came out west ten years ago, I was lucky enough to land a job with George Faraday, who's one of my partners now."

"And you've been with him ever since?" Ellen prompted.

"Just about. He was running stages up and down the Willamette Valley, in Oregon, and I worked for him until the panic of seventy-three, when he lost his business. Then I moved on. Last spring he got some backing and a partner, and he got a chance to start up a line here at Deadwood. When he asked me to come in on the deal, I didn't even consider saying no."

Walker made an actor's gesture that somehow managed to take in the camp, the gulch where they sat, and the surrounding hills, with miners working every inch of ground and every foot of stream bank. "Business should be booming."

"We're still new—pretty much a shoestring operation. Right now, of course, our stages run only as far south as Custer City. Later my partners and I hope to extend operations to Cheyenne so as to compete with the older lines—try to get a mail contract, if and when any such thing is ever awarded the Black Hills." He hesitated, touching his bristled jaw. "I work long hours. And that's why I don't always look too presentable. . . ."

Bruce Walker waved the apology aside.

Their meal arrived, homey fare but well prepared—the owners of the Grand Central had good reason to brag about their kitchen. As they ate, Tom Murdock found occasion to turn the talk away from himself. "And how are your affairs coming?" he asked. "I hear you've taken over the Bella Union."

"Only until Mr. Langrishe gets his theater finished," Ellen said. "We give our opening performance next week—on the twenty-third. We're doing *East Lynne*."

"I've never seen it," Murdock admitted. "Are you the heroine?"

"Oh, goodness, no! Claire Richards will be playing Lady Isabel. I've been cast as Barbara Hare, the second female lead. It's the first time I've ever acted . . . and I'm terrible!"

"Don't you believe her," Bruce Walker said, and Murdock saw the familiar way he laid his hand on hers and squeezed it. "She does just fine."

Ellen flashed him a smile of thanks for the assurance. To Murdock she said, "Bruce plays the villain, Francis Levison—he seduces Lady Isabel and steals her from her husband, Archibald Carlyle, and son, Willy. He takes her off to London, where they have a child. Then he abandons her and their baby in a freezing garret. Tom, you'll just hate him!"

"There's one line I've always liked especially," Walker put in. "I tap the cradle with my walking stick and ask, with the most beautiful scorn, 'And what have you named the little article, there?'" Sneering, he twirled an imaginary mustache.

Ellen continued her recital of the play's absurdities. "The baby dies, of course. Meanwhile back at East Lynne, Isabel and Archibald's son, Willy, has also been taken ill. Cindy Clevenger plays Willy," she added. "I know it's a boy's part, but she plays it anyway. . . . And Lady Isabel puts on a gray wig and a pair of blue spectacles and returns in disguise to serve as a nursemaid for her own son. Naturally, nobody recognizes her. By now there's been a divorce, and Archibald has married *me*. I hope you're following all this?" she asked anxiously.

"I—I think so." Murdock sounded dubious.

Bruce Walker suggested, "Tell him about the song."

She brightened. "Oh, yes—the song! 'Then You'll Remember Me.' You know that old one?" She hummed a phrase or two of the romantic ballad, and Murdock nodded. "Well, earlier, in Act One—before everything starts going wrong and they're still happily married and in love—there's a moment when Isabel sings this to her husband, Archibald. Now, toward the end of the play, *I'm* singing it to him— the very same song—and she comes in wearing her wig and spectacles and stands there looking upon the happy scene that once was hers. Oh, I assure you, there won't be a dry eye in the house!

"In the end Willy dies. And then Isabel dies, with Archibald's arms around her—she's taken off the spectacles, so now he knows her, and of course he forgives her for all her sins—and her dreadful mistake with Levison. Oh, Tom, you simply mustn't miss it."

"Not for anything," he assured her solemnly.

He continued with his meal, but he scarcely seemed to taste it. He listened to the bright chatter of the other two as they passed lightly over the events of the day's rehearsal, finding an endless stream of incidents and private jokes to share and find amusing. Having nothing at all to add to the conversation, with each moment Murdock felt more and more left out.

These people of the theater were a breed apart, he told himself—vital and alive, belonging to a world that was peculiarly their own—a world that someone like him could not enter. They made Tom Murdock feel by comparison like some kind of plodding workhorse, and the thought filled him with a deepening unhappiness.

For Ellen Dorsey had never appeared more attractive or more desirable than in this moment when he seemed to be watching her slip completely beyond his reach. . . .

Chapter 7

The flare-up of angry emotion on the little stage of the Bella Union, two days before the Deadwood opening, was entirely Ellen Dorsey's fault, or so she believed. She was under more severe strain than she allowed herself to show. Each step in the hurried production of *East Lynne* had elements of torturous stress, from the initial reading to the first blocking rehearsal with scripts in hand, and then—all too soon—the day came when Jack Langrishe ordered his players to lay their books aside and work entirely from memory.

This, of course, was the customary routine, long familiar to the seasoned members of the company. To Ellen it was all new and terrifying, but she would not let herself ask any special consideration just because of that. By dint of hours of study and nights of lying awake running lines in her head, she had managed to hold her own. But she feared that under such pressure, she was sure to make some bad slip, sooner or later, and disgrace herself in the eyes of the rest of the troupe. For her blunder to have happened while they were rehearsing one of the few moments of the play in which she appeared onstage with Claire Richards made it twice as humiliating.

In her role of Barbara Hare, Ellen had asked for a clandestine meeting to enlist Archibald Carlyle's aid in clearing her brother of a charge of murder—a crime actually committed by none other than the villainous Francis Levison. Their rendezvous was witnessed by Lady Isabel, who then was persuaded by Levison to interpret the meeting in the worst light. Thinking her husband a cheat, Lady Isabel would be led away in tears by Levison, to desert husband and child and flee with the scoundrel to the garrets of London.

It was just at the climactic moment during the secret rendezvous when Claire Richards and Bruce Walker were awaiting their cue to come onstage that everything suddenly stopped.

Jack Langrishe, directing from the auditorium, called impatiently, "Lines!" But whoever was supposed to be prompting the actors had apparently left his post for the moment. There was heavy silence while, still onstage, Ellen and the actor playing Archibald looked blankly at each other and at the frowning Langrishe.

At this point Claire Richards came storming out from the wings, Bruce Walker close behind her. The woman appeared coldly furious—though Ellen had to admit that even anger could not make her anything less than beautiful. She said in clipped tones, "In case anyone is interested, the line is Dorsey's. Bruce and I are back here waiting for our cue to bring us on. She's supposed to say—"

Ellen broke in, stammering. "Oh, my—my goodness! You're right—it *is* my line. I'm sorry, everybody. I just don't know what's wrong with me."

"Don't you?" the other woman retorted, turning on her. "Don't you really?" Others of the company, hearing a disturbance, were beginning to drift out from backstage to see what might be happening. Claire Richards looked at them and again at Ellen.

"Well, if no one else will tell you," she continued, more loudly and with ugly sarcasm in her voice, "I will. What's wrong with you, Miss Dorsey, is that you don't belong in a company like this! Do you realize we open day after tomorrow? It's unforgivable for anyone not to have all his lines down, cold! What do you think you're going to do when we actually get into production—when we're performing every night and trying to learn a new bill in the meantime? Perhaps you think the rest of us will *carry* you."

"I wouldn't expect anyone to do that!" Ellen insisted in anguish.

"Well, you can be sure no one's going to. We're all

professionals here, who've learned we can depend on one another. It's simply not fair that some *amateur*—"

"Claire! That's enough!"

It was Jack Langrishe who broke in and silenced her. He had got to his feet, and his voice filled the tiny auditorium, bringing every eye to him. Plainly, he was angry. He told his leading actress sternly, "I would hope I needn't remind you that it's not professional to disrupt a rehearsal with a screaming fit! If there are any complaints about the way this company is being managed, they can be taken up with me—in private! Is that understood? By everyone?"

A numbed silence greeted the uncharacteristic rebuke. Bruce Walker looked very disturbed, and he ventured to protest, "Jack, she didn't mean any of this. I think the truth is, we're all of us on edge about opening in a brand new camp."

Claire Richards turned her fury on him. "I'll not have *you* apologize for me!" Her face had gone white; in her voice was a hint of hysteria. "Get away and let me alone."

"Claire, please!" Bruce tried to put a hand on her arm, but she jerked free and actually tried to strike him. Avoiding the blow, he caught at her hand and managed to trap both her wrists. There was a silent struggle then as she fought with him, breathing hard, her dark and lustrous hair falling down from its pins.

"Enough of this!" Jack Langrishe shook his head. Then he said in weary resignation, "We all need a break— fifteen minutes. We'll pick up again with the next scene. . . ."

Ellen didn't wait for him to finish. She turned and stumbled blindly down the few shallow steps from stage level to the floor of the theater. No one called after her or tried to stop her; she would have paid no heed if they had. She hurried past the rows of crude benches that had been set up in place of the gaming tables, then continued across the dance floor. Tiny, curtained box seats—where the girls of the Bella Union would normally take their men for private drinking—formed a horseshoe around the rear of the hall. The street door was back there, too, and Ellen made for it.

Blinded by the beginning of tears, she found the latch and fumbled it open, went through, and pulled the door shut behind her. The warm sun struck her face; the sounds and smells of the street engulfed her. Her back against the crude panel door of the theater, her head bowed, Ellen fought to regain control of her emotions. All she felt was the need to escape from that dreadful, humiliating encounter with Claire Richards—to be completely alone, long enough to get control of herself.

The chance to join the Langrishe troupe had seemed a heaven-sent opportunity she couldn't refuse. Now that it was too late, in this bitter moment, she wondered if it wasn't the worst mistake she could have made.

Her efforts to fit in with the company appeared to have come to nothing. She had only been a disruptive element—the rankest amateur, as Claire Richards had called her, totally out of place in a company of seasoned performers. But now there was no way out. She was trapped, and the company was stuck with her. . . .

So you'll have to make the best of it, Ellen Dorsey told herself sternly. *Take yourself back in there and face them!* She brought out a handkerchief from a pocket of her blouse, dabbed at her cheeks, and blew her nose. It was only when she had put the handkerchief away again that she became aware of the man.

She smelled the whiskey on him, first. She looked up and saw him looming over her—saw the unshaven whiskers, the red-rimmed eyes, and the loose grin. When he spoke, his words spilled out in a nearly incoherent mumble, but she didn't have any need of an interpreter—his meaning was all too clear. His breath against her face was making her sick. She shook her head and told him curtly, "Go away. Please!"

The man only grinned more broadly, showing his yellow teeth. "Aw, come on, now!" he urged, more loudly. "I like you fine. I can see you're real class, not like what's in them cribs down in the Badlands." He gave a jerk of his head toward the foot of Main Street where, Ellen had learned from gossip, Deadwood's red-light district was located. The man pawed at her sleeve, but in revulsion her arm pulled free, and she slid away from him along the closed door, reaching behind her for the latch.

His grin suddenly faded. Slapping the palm of a hand against the door, he leaned against it, cutting off retreat and bringing his face close again to hers. All at once he turned angry. "Now, cut that out! You ain't going nowhere. You don't think you can get rid of me that easy!"

At that moment she was overwhelmed by the realization that even a scream would do little good on this street and in this town; in any event, her throat had gone too dry for a sound to emerge. Really frightened now, unable to move, she stared into the bloodshot eyes so near her own.

That was when a hand seized the man by a shoulder. It appeared merely to rest there, but from the way the man winced and then began to squirm, Ellen knew that it was doing more than that. A howl of pain broke from him, and after that he was spinning clumsily away from Ellen, crying out, "Dammit, take your damn paw off of—"

But when the drunk saw what man stood coldly eyeing him, his words broke off and he stared.

Ellen stared, as well. She knew who this tall, fair-haired man with the downward-sweeping mustache must be even before the drunk stammered his name: "H-Hickok!" It was his turn to go limp with obvious terror. "Golly, Bill, you took me by surprise! I never meant—"

The tall man cut short this slurred speech, saying, "I only allow my friends to call me Bill, mister—and you ain't one of them. Now, if you know what's good for you, you'll get away from here . . . *and let the lady be!*"

"Sure! Sure, Bill—uh—Mr. Hickok. Whatever you say!" And with that the fellow backed away and went scampering off, glad to have escaped.

Hickok turned to Ellen, who said quickly, "I do thank you, sir. I was scared half to death!"

"I'm real sorry, miss," he told her. "It pays to be careful in a rough camp like this one. But he won't bother you again, is my guess." He added, "My name is James Hickok. Some folks call me Wild Bill, though."

She had heard about the famous Wild Bill Hickok being in Deadwood, and the description would scarcely have fit anyone else. She also had heard that he spent much of his time at his favorite card table in the No. 10 Saloon, next to the Bella Union.

As if reading her thoughts, the tall man nodded and said, "I'm glad now I happened to step out for a breath of air just when I did. I take it you're one of the actors. . . ."

"I'm Ellen Dorsey. As for being an actor," she said ruefully, "I'm afraid there's a good deal of doubt about that. . . . But I'm with the company, yes."

"That's real interesting. You wouldn't know it to look at me, but I was in theater once."

"Is that a fact? No, I didn't know."

"Trod the boards, I think they call it, with a couple of my old chums, Buffalo Bill Cody and Texas Jack Omohundro. That would be—oh, three or four years ago. Somebody wrote us a play all about our Indian scouting days, and we went on tour with it back east for about six months. Lots of people came to see us, but I'm afraid I wasn't really cut out to be—what do they call it?—a thespian. Anyway, we broke up the outfit. Right now I'm a married man, and I got to be thinking about settling down somewhere. So I ain't likely to try anything like *that* ever again!"

Looking at him, she thought that with all his size and bearing he must have cut a very impressive figure on a stage. But unfortunately that wasn't always enough.

Gallantly, he added, "But I ain't that soured on the whole idea of going into a playhouse again as a spectator. I'm looking forward to the opening of this one."

"Thank you. I hope you won't be disappointed."

"Oh, I'm cer—" Hickok's answer was interrupted by a shout hailing him, and they turned to look at the figure striding up the hill in their direction carrying a Winchester repeating rifle. The call had come from a rather small fellow—or a boy, Ellen thought at the first glance—but something about the person inside the dirty fringed buckskins seemed noticeably wrong for that. The newcomer shouted Hickok's name again, and then the flat-crowned hat was pushed back, and Ellen saw that this was, beyond any doubt, a woman.

Her hair was pulled up and tucked under the hat. At a closer look, she appeared to be quite young, perhaps twenty-six or thereabout, but her skin had been burned dark and leathery, and her rather plain features were already beginning to coarsen. She carried herself with a masculine swagger, her voice booming loudly as she grinned widely and said, "How about it, Bill? You gonna stand me to a drink?" She jerked a thumb toward the nearby saloon.

Glancing at Hickok, Ellen saw the clear distaste with which he regarded this creature. He quickly shook his head. "There ain't time," he said flatly. "I've got a game waiting."

"Oh, sure," the young woman said. She didn't seem to be troubled by his refusal. "I know you—you *always* got a game going someplace. Who's this?" she demanded in her bold and carrying voice as she turned her attention to Ellen. "Don't look to me like any of Tom Miller's girls."

"She's no dance-hall girl, Calamity," he said curtly. "She's a lady—something I don't suppose you'd know much about."

"Oh, hell!" the woman said. "I guess I know a lady when I see one. I been chased out of towns by some of the best!" With a tug at Hickok's arm, she urged, "Come on now, Bill. How about that drink?"

"No!" He jerked loose, with a look of utter scorn. Not speaking another word, he wheeled about and, stiffly erect with his handsome head arrogantly lifted, strode back into the saloon.

Ellen Dorsey could say nothing at all, but the other woman let loose a heartfelt swear word, then exclaimed, "Well, how do you like that! Talk about giving somebody the cold shoulder. You'd never know, would you, we'd been together all the way to Deadwood. . . ."

"Together?" the word was startled out of Ellen. Inadvertently, she felt her cheeks start to grow warm, and her reaction drew an amused glance.

"Not like that! All I meant was, in the same wagon train. I better shut up before I say something to shock you even worse. I never did know how to talk to no lady."

"Oh, please," Ellen interjected, "don't worry about

that. I'm not sure what constitutes a lady, but despite what Mr. Hickok said, I certainly never thought of myself as being one. In fact, I know people who'd say I was nothing but an entertainer."

Something appeared to click. "So *that's* it! You must be one of them theater people, right? An actor."

Remembering the awful scene at rehearsal, Ellen shook her head. "I only wish I could believe that. I just hope I can do better as a singer. My name's Ellen Dorsey," she added, offering her hand.

Her new acquaintance shook it as vigorously as a man would. "Pleased to meetcha. I'm Jane—mostly called Calamity, on account of that's what people get who try messing with me!" She patted her rifle, boasting, "I can outshoot and outcuss most any man I ever met up with."

And outdrink them? Ellen Dorsey wondered. The brazen woman went on before the actress had time to comment.

"I've Injun-guided for the military, and I can boss a bull team with the best of 'em. I'd sure like to be pretty as you, though. And I really got to hand it to anybody that can sing," she added with a hint of wistfulness. "I was born Martha Jane Canary, but in spite of my name I can't even carry a tune—got a croak that'd more'n likely shame a crow! I'm gonna make a point of coming to hear you."

"I hope you do," the other woman said impulsively, and meant it. This queer creature, with her tough manner and brash tongue, had something forthright and direct about her that made Ellen add, "I'd like to be friends."

"You would?" Calamity Jane stared at Ellen as though finding her hard to believe. She frowned then and said, on a serious note, "I guess you never been in a place like Deadwood, have you?"

"No. And—it's kind of frightening."

Calamity patted Ellen's arm with her dirty and callused fingers. "You'll be all right. Sure you will! There's a lot of rough stuff goes on—and a lot of people like me, that you likely ain't had to deal with before. But if anybody tries to give you trouble, you just let ol' Calamity know about it!"

At that, Ellen had to laugh aloud. "I surely will . . . if I can find you."

"Oh, I ain't too hard to find—not in a little ol' camp that ain't no bigger than this one. I generally make a lot of noise wherever I happen to be. Too much, some would say." She took off her battered hat, beat dust from it against her buckskin pants, and added, "Well, I best be moseyin'. Miss, I hope you never know what it's like to have a thirst like the one I got ridin' me now. Maybe Bill Hickok won't buy me a drink, but I can always find one of the boys who'll be more'n happy to. Me and the boys—we get along fine." She stuck out her hand again. "Good luck, Miss Dorsey. I really mean it."

Ellen took the hand with a smile. "I wish the same to you, Jane."

A *strange person*, she thought as she watched Jane go swaggering up the street in search of drinking companions. A queer product of the frontier, loud and tough, yet for all her faults, Ellen doubted that Calamity Jane had a streak of real meanness in her, anywhere. She wondered idly if they really would be meeting again.

Suddenly she became aware again of the sights and sounds and smells of Deadwood surrounding her as she stood there in front of the Bella Union: the passage of traffic through the crooked street; the hubbub of voices and the stuttering racket of hammers putting up frame buildings to replace the dirty canvas of the camp's original tents; the mingling scents of woodsmoke and pine shavings, of whiskey and damp sawdust issuing from the No. 10, and the dry dust lifting in a cloud from under the hooves and wheels of a bull train being shouted onward by its whip-wielding drivers.

Her encounter with Hickok and the drunk and with Calamity Jane had almost put thought of the disastrous rehearsal from her mind; by now, though, more than fifteen minutes must surely have passed, and so, reluctantly, Ellen went back inside to face whatever awaited her. She was reaching for the latch when the door opened and Jack Langrishe exclaimed, "Oh—here you are! I was just coming to look for you."

"Oh, Mr. Langrishe . . ." The door closed behind, shutting them into the dark entryway. From the little auditorium beyond came the voices of the actors, working through a scene. "I want to apologize," Ellen told him, "to you—to the whole company—for what happened there on the stage. It was my fault . . . all of it!"

"Because you missed a cue?" His homely comedian's features could turn almost beautiful when he smiled the way he did now. "Believe me, there isn't a one of us who hasn't blacked out on his lines—a lot more times than once. And that includes, I might add, our temperamental leading lady."

"But it's not the same thing!" she protested. "All the rest of you have worked together a long time. By now you're practically a family. And as she says, I'm an amateur—an intruder. If I have any hope of being accepted, I just can't afford to make mistakes."

"That, my dear, if you'll pardon my saying so"—and his smile took away the sting of the word—"is nonsense. Remember, it concerns me just as much as you that this troupe should remain a happy family. I knew perfectly well what I was doing when I engaged you. I have to be a judge of people. I never doubted, from that one interview, that you were a fine young woman and the whole company would come to love and accept you—the way they already have."

"I'm afraid we both know that's not true."

Jack Langrishe sighed. "Claire, you mean." He shook his head. "I must admit I don't know what could have got into that woman. . . . I've just finished trying to talk to her, but she's put up a wall that I simply can't get past."

"Mr. Langrishe—" she began, but then she couldn't finish. Jack Langrishe had a right to know the cause of any dissension within his company, but it was hardly a newcomer's place to reveal the secret that Claire Richards had already refused to tell him herself. It was disturbing enough to feel that Bruce Walker's interest in her was the real cause of the friction with Claire, while at the same time, she had to admit that she enjoyed his attentions and was very far from wanting them to stop. . . .

To herself she said bitterly, *Ellen, you're a coward!* But to Langrishe she could only say, as he looked at her questioningly, "I—I forget what I was going to say."

She felt guilty when he placed his hand on her shoulder in a gentle and understanding manner, and said, "I know. You're upset. But you're not alone—I think we're all more tense than we realize over this particular opening. We shouldn't be needing you for another half hour or so. Why don't you go back to the cot in the dressing room and try to get some rest while you can."

"Thank you," she said lamely. "Perhaps I will."

Watching her go, Jack Langrishe frowned thoughtfully. There were things going on here that he didn't know about . . . and of all the problems that confronted a theatrical manager—the constant shortage of money, the difficulties of setting up in a new place, the uncertainties of local feuds and politics—of all these, none were more troublesome than the hostilities that could arise between people as varied and strong-willed as a troupe of actors. "Perhaps I've been at this too long," he said aloud. "How old am I? Only forty-five? And still broke! Good Lord, just now I feel ripe enough to play King Lear."

Behind him the street door opened suddenly, letting a blast of sunlight into the vestibule. When he turned, he saw silhouetted a pair of figures. "Yes . . . ? Is there something I can do for you?"

The newcomers stepped inside, and now he could make them out more clearly. The man was tall, rawboned, and clean shaven. His companion was a well-dressed woman; in Langrishe's opinion she would have been quite handsome except for an indefinable hint of anxiety about her eyes. On her hand, which rested in the crook of the man's elbow, was a plain gold band.

"You're Jack Langrishe?" the man asked, and waited for a nod of affirmation. "The name is Varnes—I'm a local businessman."

"I believe I've heard of you."

What the director had heard was another matter—an unflattering description of a gambling-hall operator whose games lay under a cloud of suspicion. But Varnes could probably buy Jack Langrishe and his company a couple of times over: Someone like that needed to be treated with wary respect. The director waited.

"This is Pearl, my wife." Langrishe nodded politely as Varnes continued, "Pearl's the reason we're here. She's crazy about the theater—attended all the time while we were in Frisco—but she hasn't had much of a chance since. So she's all excited about you people being in Deadwood—been pestering me to bring her down, find out if she could look around a bit . . . maybe watch you rehearse."

"Is that a fact?" It struck Langrishe oddly that she looked considerably more frightened than eager; she offered not a word. Something, he thought, was definitely wrong. But he told them, with a nod toward the auditorium where the voices from the stage could be heard, "We're having rehearsal now. You're both welcome."

"Thanks," Johnny Varnes said curtly, and steered his wife through the vestibule. Langrishe closed the street door they had left open and followed.

The stage of the Bella Union wasn't very impressive, with only a shallow stage, though it did have a curtain and a row of reflector footlights. The company's props and drop curtains had not yet arrived from Denver, but Langrishe was used to making do with whatever was available. Claire Richards and Bruce Walker were alone onstage now, and the director was pleased to see that his leading lady appeared to have settled down and was again behaving in a professional manner. To the visitors he said, "If you'd care to see what it's like backstage, I'd be glad to have someone show you around."

"Not me, thanks," Johnny Varnes said. "Pearl's the one for that sort of thing. I'll just stay out here. In fact, I'd like a few words with you. . . ."

"All right." Langrishe called to Bertie Clevenger, who had just come through the backstage door. He made introductions and explained what was wanted. Giving the Varnes woman a warm smile, Bertie led her away, chatting in a way that should have put even the most timid stranger at ease. Once they had gone, the gambler brought out a cigar case and offered his host a smoke, afterward lighting up for them both.

"Well, Langrishe." Varnes spoke around his cigar as he puffed it to life. The director waited, attending critically to what was happening on the stage. At the same time he missed nothing in the gambler's face, which appeared hawkish under the skylights in the ceiling overhead. At last Varnes went on, "I'm really impressed. And I understand you're putting up your own theater."

"The work on it is going a bit slow, as yet," Langrishe said, evasively. He wasn't ready to admit to anyone how badly his shortage of cash was hampering him.

"There's something you should give some thought to. . . . This is a tough camp—some rather violent things go on at times. I'd hate to think of anything really bad happening here at the Bella Union—say, on opening night."

Jack Langrishe felt a cold warning begin to move along his spine. His reply, however, was quiet and controlled. "I've played tough camps before, Mr. Varnes. I've managed to hold my own."

"Glad to hear that. Still—" Varnes removed the cigar from his mouth to study the burning end. "You never know. There can always be a first time, when matters get completely out of control. On the other hand, there are steps a person can take ahead of time—sort of insurance, if you understand what I mean."

"I'm beginning to think I do," Langrishe said coldly. "But go ahead."

"As it happens, I have men working for me, and others that I can get, who are among the most dangerous in camp—that is, if you should get on the wrong side of them. What I'm prepared to offer you—"

Jack Langrishe had heard enough. He interpreted angrily, "I think you're offering me the rare privilege of paying you money to keep me on the *right* side. And if I *don't* pay, then at the opening, day after tomorrow, I can look for the worst to happen. Isn't that what you're really saying?"

Eyes like nailheads looked at him from Johnny Varnes's bony face. "You put words in my mouth, Langrishe!"

"If so, it's because I'm thoroughly familiar with the script," Langrishe retorted. "Believe me, Mr. Varnes, I've heard all this dialogue before. I understand now that you only brought your wife here this afternoon as an excuse so you could read it to me again. Well, I'm afraid I'm not interested in listening to any more of it."

"No?" Their looks met and clashed. The gambler's thin lips quirked. He said harshly, in a way that left no uncertainty between them, "You may come to wish you *had* listened. . . . Pearl!"

At the tone of his voice, everything stopped. Rehearsal forgotten, the people on the stage stood and watched in silence as Pearl Varnes, who had just returned with Bertie Clevenger from their brief tour backstage, joined her husband. Not another word was spoken, though Johnny Varnes gave Langrishe a final, meaningful stare.

Then he turned and followed his wife from the Bella Union. He left the street door standing wide open behind them.

Chapter 8

Polk Renner, inspecting the stage route with his boss, reined in his horse and said, "Listen!"

Murdock pulled up alongside, scanned the land below, and nodded. A strengthening ground wind from the north brought to them—along with its pine scent and dust—a sporadic rattle of gunfire somewhere ahead. "That should be just about at Kemp's Station."

"You really think they've gone and ambushed a *station*?" Renner stared at him. "What the hell would that get them?"

"Let's find out. . . ." The two men rode off.

A fledgling stage line like Murdock's, operating on a close budget, could hardly afford to build and equip all the stations it needed. Instead, arrangements were made to use facilities already standing along the trail between Deadwood and Custer City, as at Anderson's. Kemp's was another such station. Joe Kemp was a farmer—a stubborn farmer. Having followed the first wave of stampeders into the Black Hills, he had found a pocket of land that he liked and, no longer interested in the elusive gleam of gold, had put up a house and barn and then cleared and tilled a couple of acres for corn and root crops. The fees paid him by Tom Murdock and his partners in the Deadwood Stage Line were a convenient source of cash.

Sooner or later, Joe Kemp insisted, the government was going to have to declare all this country open for white settlement, and when it did, he would already be here, with his claim staked. Meanwhile, he refused to be bothered by any warnings that the Sioux, after their triumph at the Little Big Horn in June, might decide the time was ripe for killing or driving out all the intruders from their sacred land. Just let them try, he was fond of saying—they'd find Joe Kemp damned hard to drive! He figured he could put his land to better use than any Indian.

Renner was thinking of such boasts now as he halted next to Murdock and said gruffly, "Maybe Joe could've been *too* sure of himself."

Not answering, Murdock looked over the scene below where the timber crowded in around Kemp's holdings. These consisted of a house and barn, built of poles and roofed with wooden shingles, a corral containing half a dozen relay horses for the stage line, and a stake-and-rider fence around his cultivated land. Just now a hoe was leaning against the fence where someone had apparently abandoned it in the midst of interrupted labor.

A little distance from the main building was a stage-coach, also looking as if it had been abandoned. It stood with its brake on and with both doors gaping wide, just the way the passengers had left them. The team was still in harness, but the reins lay on the ground. The horses were stirring, moving helplessly about in their traces, terrorized by the continuing racket of firing guns. And on the high front seat, the figure of a man slumped motionless, one leather ribbon still clutched in his lifeless hand.

"Damn!" Polk Renner exclaimed in angry shock. "Oh, dammit, Tom! That's Brownie—one of the best drivers I ever rode with. I've owed him ten dollars for the past three months. . . . He hardly ever mentioned it."

Murdock nodded grimly but said nothing. His attention was riveted to the scene below as he tried to sort out what had happened. The picture was reasonably clear. The raiders must have hit the stage somewhere north of here, sending it into a race for the haven of the station. Brown, the driver, hadn't quite made it to safety; presumably the passengers and the guard had been luckier. Murdock wondered if the strongbox had been rescued or was still stowed away in the boot.

From the edge of the trees below and to their left, what sounded like half a dozen repeating rifles were working over the station building. From inside the station came return fire, but it sounded as though no more than one or two of the occupants had rifles. Murdock also heard the flatter popping of handguns coming from inside, but at that range, he was thinking, they could hardly be effective. Obviously the attackers knew this, too: They were being careless about showing themselves.

Just now one stepped out into clear view from the shadows of the timber screen. Tom Murdock had a distinct glimpse of a brown body, naked except for buckskin breeches. The figure carried a rifle, and Tom saw him trigger a quick bullet at the house before fading back from sight.

At Murdock's elbow Polk Renner said harshly, "By God, an Indian! Looks like they're after the horses. Or do you suppose they're making one of the first moves to try and take their hills back?"

His boss didn't bother with speculating. He had made a quick strategy decision, and now he said, "I want you to work your way over there behind them." He indicated the timbered hillside just above the attackers. "If they give you a target, shoot and try to get them confused—but don't you go giving *them* one. You hear?"

Renner nodded. "I hear." Pulling his Winchester from the saddle scabbard, he said, frowning, "And what about you?"

"I'm going down."

"Down there?"

"I'll be all right."

Clearly reluctant, Renner followed these orders after a moment's hesitation, shaking his head as he reined his horse off through the thin stand of trees. When he was gone, Tom Murdock unholstered his gun and checked the action. He spoke to his mount then and started easing it down the slope, gun ready, and listening to catch any change in the sporadic rhythm of gunfire.

Where the timber began to thin and the slope leveled off, he dismounted and, tying the reins to a pine limb, proceeded on foot. He reached the edge of the trees; the motionless stagecoach with its frantic team was directly before him, Joe Kemp's buildings lying beyond. As he watched, gunpowder smoke blossomed at the windows, to scatter on the breeze that carried away the popping of gunshot.

Murdock sank to one knee, seeking the screen of a clump of bushes. He was barely in time, for at that moment a couple of the attackers broke into the open and began moving—on foot and crouching to make smaller targets—in the direction of the house. One of them carried a rifle, the other a handgun. Murdock could have fired a shot at them, but they were still moving, and so he held off—he was curious to learn what the pair were up to. The rifle fire from the timber had suddenly redoubled, as though to draw the attention of the people in the house and keep them occupied.

The two dark-skinned, partially clad figures were soon shielded from the house by the bulky shape of the stalled stagecoach, and Murdock was not too surprised to see that this appeared to be their goal. But now they were passing farther out of good six-shooter range. Murdock came to his feet and started after them; it was time to make his move.

The Indian with the pistol had reached the coach, and he went up the high front wheel while the other waited below, hurriedly scanning out the open ground around them. It was he who caught sight of Tom Murdock, coming toward them at a run. Murdock sensed the man's startled reaction. As though only then remembering the rifle he carried by the balance, the Indian whipped it up and fired a shot.

There was a white flash and a puff of smoke, but the bullet missed. The rifleman threw a fresh shell in the chamber, but Murdock wasn't giving him a second chance. The stage-line owner came to a halt and, bracing his gun hand with the other, took careful aim. He fired; the gun barrel kicked upward, and as he lowered it again he saw the rifleman collapsing into the dust with his weapon.

The other Indian was now on the high seat of the stage and, after shoving aside the limp body of the driver, was hurriedly rummaging in the boot. When he heard the exchange of shots, he straightened and saw Murdock. This man had quicker reflexes than his partner, and suddenly a bullet from the pistol he held gouged up the dirt in front of Murdock's boot.

The stage owner held steady, boots set, smoking revolver still braced in front of him, ready to fire. When he did, the gun bucked against his hand, and while the terrified stage horses squealed and fought the brake, the man on the driver's seat was knocked backward, tumbling in a slow fall over the side of the coach.

At that moment a new weapon, which had to be Polk Renner's Winchester, opened up from somewhere on the wooded ridge opposite the station buildings. He must have found a target, Murdock thought. At the unexpected onslaught from the rear, the remaining attackers' guns fell silent. Renner hammered out three more shots in quick succession, and then he, too, held off.

Everything had suddenly gone wrong for the raiders, and with two of them lying dead beside the stagecoach, the rest had apparently decided it was time to quit. As Murdock stood listening, he heard the sound of several horses starting to gallop, but it faded quickly, a few scattered hoofbeats coming back as they hit a stretch of bare rock. Then all the noise of retreat was blotted up by the timber.

One glance at the pair he had shot convinced Murdock they were finished. Two men dead that had been alive a moment ago—and at his hand! It was a sobering realization, something he would rather put from his mind if he could. Now, with the shooting over, men came rushing from the house—Joe Kemp himself, the guard off the coach whose name was Ted Norton, three more who looked like passengers, and another man, who was a stock handler for the stage line.

While the last man hurried to settle the frightened teams, which in their frenzy were still straining at the harness, Murdock swung up on the coach's wheel to have a look at the driver. The brief examination merely confirmed what he already knew: Brown was dead. A pair of bullets had found him.

Still intact in the boot under the driver's seat was the box of gold dust that had cost Brown his life.

"Give me a hand," Murdock shouted down to Norton over the excited voices. Brown had been wire tough but of no great weight. It was not too difficult to pass his limp, bloody form down to Ted Norton's outstretched arms. Leaving the strongbox where it was for the time being, Tom Murdock dropped to the ground just as Polk Renner rode up, leading a couple of horses with empty saddles.

"The rest of the attackers took off," he said in answer to Murdock's questioning look. "These horses got left behind. Must belong to these two." He indicated the raiders his boss had killed.

"Did you hit any of them?" Murdock asked.

"No. Scared 'em was all." He added bleakly, "I only hope one of these two was the bastard that got Brownie!"

He dismounted to join the group, some with guns dangling in their hands, staring at the dead men on the ground. Joe Kemp, a stoop-shouldered man with gray hair and skin burned brick red and peeling, spoke for the rest when he asked, "Why the hell would a bunch of Indians chase a stagecoach—almost up to the front door?"

Instead of answering, Tom Murdock went down on one knee beside the dark-skinned man he had shot off the front boot. With distaste, he took hold of the man's shoulder and flopped him over onto his back, turning the slack face and sightless eyes to the sun. He looked at the man for a long, silent moment; then, from a pocket, he pulled out a handkerchief and, taking a handful of hair to hold the head steady, used the cloth to wipe the man's face clean. Someone swore. Whatever stain had been used, it came away easily enough, turning the handkerchief a dark brown.

"Hell!" Polk Renner exclaimed. "He's *white!*"

"Look closer," Murdock suggested grimly, and pointed to the narrow ridge of scar tissue that he had uncovered, angling across the forehead and puckering the cheek below it. "We've met him before. His name—"

"I know it like I know my own!" Renner interrupted. "It's Bart Ryan. . . ."

The other dead bandit proved on examination to be no more an Indian than Ryan, but the face was not one that anybody recognized—merely another in the floating population of toughs that had infested these hills in the wake of the rush for gold. Ted Norton, the shotgun guard, shook his head as he looked at the pair.

"So it *was* the shipment they wanted after all," he said. "I swear I couldn't figure why an Indian would be after us, unless maybe to grab off the horses—or just to lift some scalps. Certainly there was nothing Indians could want with a box of gold dust. But in any case they really put the heat on us—but Brownie wouldn't quit. Even with a bullet in him, he gave 'em a chase clear to the door of the station before they were able to finish him off."

"He was a good man," Tom Murdock agreed soberly. "A damn shame it had to happen. And it leaves me with a run to finish—and no driver."

At once the stock handler, a young fellow named Homer Reese who had been busy trying to quiet the horses, was there next to his boss. "Let *me* take it through, Mr. Murdock!" He was nearly stammering in his eagerness. "I've done some driving. This is a chance I've wanted ever since I went to work for you!"

Murdock looked questioningly at Joe Kemp, who slowly nodded and said, "I got an idea the boy can handle it, Tom. I take it he's had experience. One thing's sure, he really knows his horses."

Though he was young and rather slender, Murdock thought Reese had the hands and the shoulders to manage a four-horse team and to keep them in their collars. "Well, you look like my only choice. All right, Homer. Get some fresh horses on that rig and get ready to roll for Custer City. Remember, you're carrying the strongbox. I'll expect a report on your performance from Ted Norton. You finish this run to suit him, and we'll talk about a regular job as a driver."

"Yes, *sir*!"

The young fellow hurried off about this work as though afraid Murdock might change his mind. Turning back to Joe Kemp, Murdock asked, "Can you handle things alone until I can send you a new stock handler?"

"I can manage. What about Brownie? He was a damn fine man . . . and a good friend. He had no family anywhere, no next of kin. Say, there's a spot right here on my land—a little hill with some trees on it—where I'd kind of like to see him put to rest. That is, if you don't think of something better."

"Sounds fine to me," Murdock said. "I know he'd appreciate you feeling that way about it."

"But the others," Kemp went on with sour distaste, "the ones that done him in—I got no room at all for such as them."

"Never mind," Murdock told him. "I got other plans for those two. Get me a length of rope and something to wrap them in. . . ."

Murdock and Renner were well on their way again, heading toward Deadwood, when Polk finally brought up a question that he had been cogitating on for some time. "Tom," he said suddenly, "I don't feel easy about all this. I mean, Ryan is dead, and he *was* the one that held us up before . . . but I got a creepin' suspicion our troubles ain't over yet. What do you think?"

The question came as a welcome break in Murdock's train of thought. He had been morbidly pondering the stiffening, blanket-wrapped shapes of his victims, now lashed to the saddles of the abandoned horses to accompany Renner and him back to town. Every day in Deadwood, Murdock rubbed elbows with men to whom killing came easily, men who could take a life without a moment's remorse. He hated the thought that he might become one of those men.

Now taking his mind from such bleak matters, he offered an answer to Polk Renner's query. "I honestly think that Johnny Varnes is the man behind these holdups. You'll remember he talked pretty big—and yet, for all that, he may have decided we were getting a little too close on his trail. We may have worried him some. Enough to make him toss in a fake Indian scare in hopes of mixing us up. At least that's one explanation."

"I hope you're right," Renner said. "It would be nice to think we made the bastard lose a little sleep."

Toward sundown they came over the hump, and the

rough stage road dropped away to become Deadwood's Main Street. Clouds were flaming like fire above the timber-stripped western ridges as the sun sank behind them. By mutual agreement, Renner and Murdock rode directly to the big tented saloon.

The usual hubbub spilled out through its open front. Before the entrance, a number of loiterers came quickly alert as they saw the stiff, shrouded figures tied onto the two unmounted horses. One lantern-jawed man, leaning against a roof pole and chewing on a matchstick, straightened and called out, "Hey mister! What you got there?"

Drawing rein, Tom Murdock answered briefly. "A present for Johnny Varnes. You go tell him."

If the man resented being given orders, his curiosity—and the hint of possible excitement—overrode it. His eyes sharpened with interest. "Yeah!" He tossed the matchstick away and turned quickly into the tent.

Waiting, Murdock dismounted and, walking to one of the other horses, proceeded to unlash the ropes that held Bart Ryan's blanket-wrapped body. Seeing this, Polk Renner quickly duplicated his actions on the other corpse. Without ceremony, and ignoring the stares of the onlookers, Murdock and Renner dumped the already stiff bodies to the ground in front of the tent and, taking hold of the blankets' edges, rolled the corpses out onto the ground. A few of the onlookers gasped, and someone cried, "Indians! You were attacked by Indians!" But then Murdock's messenger reappeared, only to be shoved aside unceremoniously as Creed Dunning strode out past him.

Johnny Varnes's right-hand man stared at the bodies, then lifted a furious glare at Murdock. "What the hell is this?"

Murdock retorted coldly, "I sent for your boss—not you."

"Well, he ain't here. It's *me* you're dealing with. And I want to know—"

"Take a look," Murdock invited. "Here's two of your men masquerading as Indians. One of them is that scar-faced bastard!" Bending over, he braced up Bart Ryan's face, its dark stain only half removed—but enough to reveal, clearly, the telltale scar.

There could be no mistaking the shock in Creed Dunning's reaction. He stiffened, his eyes widening, and then shot a furious look at Murdock, who went on smoothly, "You can tell Johnny the trick didn't work—that is, in case he hasn't already heard from the ones that got away alive. And while you're at it, let him know that after this, any more thieves I get my hands on will likewise be dumped on his doorstep. I know for a fact that this is where they come from." He nodded to Polk Renner, and the two of them stepped back to their horses and mounted.

"Hold on a minute!" Creed Dunning had recovered enough to shout at them as they started to rein away. "You ain't leaving them here!"

Tom Murdock looked at him, blandly smiling, and retorted, "Why not? They're yours. . . ."

They left without a backward look, and as voices began to rise in back of them, Polk Renner said with grim satisfaction, "I guess we got no doubts left. That look on his face was all the proof anybody could need."

"It's enough for me, at least." Tom Murdock moved his shoulders as though to ease the burden of the day's happenings, then added in a different tone, "Right now we got better things to think about. Let's go find something to eat and get ourselves cleaned up."

Polk Renner exclaimed, "By golly, you're right. I almost forgot why it was we made such a point of getting back to Deadwood tonight: We're spendin' the evening at the theater!"

Chapter 9

Jack Langrishe was satisfied that they were going to have a good house. He had taken up his position early in front of the Bella Union, where oil flares announced the night's opening. There he paced and watched as the first trickle of patrons grew to a steady stream. He nodded and returned an occasional greeting, all the while mentally tabulating the gate. He was not really surprised at the impressive total—in a camp like Deadwood, where so many footloose men had gold dust in their pockets and little else but whores and booze and gambling to spend it on, any novelty was almost sure to draw a crowd—enough of one, at least, to fill the hall of the Bella Union.

He saw too many guns, but he frowned and let them pass, knowing that to own and wear a sidearm was an accepted custom among the inhabitants of a place like this. All the same, the sight of so many weapons being carried into the hall reminded him, all too strongly, of the threat from Johnny Varnes.

Of Varnes himself he had seen no sign, nor of his wife—who seemed a rather nice person, according to the women of the troupe who had shown her around on that afternoon two days ago. They had found Pearl Varnes to be a timid and gentle woman, pathetically grateful for any attention. Despite her reputed interest in the theatrical art, however, it began to look as though she might miss tonight's opening, after all. It occurred to him that this could be by design: If Varnes meant to disrupt tonight's performance, he probably wouldn't want his wife to be on hand.

He checked the time again, snapped his watchcase

shut, and slipped it into his vest pocket as he turned, at last, to enter the theater. The hubbub of voices from the hall struck him full in the face: An old-time actor's pulse never failed to quicken at that exciting, if intimidating, sound. At a table set up just inside the vestibule, two male members of the company sat taking in admission, with a cigar box for cash and a glass jar for those who paid in dust from their leather pouches. Bruce Walker, already in costume though not as yet made up for his role as the villain, gave his director a wink and said, "We're really pulling it in. If this keeps up, you might even be able to pay us something on our salaries!"

Langrishe ignored that. He asked, "Notice any dangerous-looking characters?"

Walker, with an airy wave of the hand, indicated the noise from the crowd that packed the hall. "In *this* camp, they all look dangerous to me."

Not wanting to add to his company's normal anxiety about an opening night, Langrishe had said nothing to them about the threat from Johnny Varnes. He continued to keep his own counsel, saying only, "I'll be going backstage now for a cheering word with the company. You two stay and take care of the stragglers for another twenty minutes or so. Just be sure to mind your entrances."

The handsome Walker flashed him the confident smile that had caused hearts to flutter at many a matinee. "I've never missed an entrance cue in my life," he assured the director. "Have no fear. I'll be on hand to work my foul will on the lovely Isabel!"

Langrishe went on into the hall.

The crowd was noisy but appeared to be in a good mood; with a showman's experience, he judged it safe to let them wait a spell longer. By now almost every bench was full, and there was considerable milling about, with men leaning from the horseshoe of curtained boxes and shouting to acquaintances on the floor. The audience contained only a scattering of women—wives of Deadwood merchants, he supposed, and a few others the men had brought along from the cribs and sporting houses. The reflectored oil lamps that served as footlights were as yet unlighted; to one side of the tiny stage an upright piano stood waiting—the only one that Langrishe knew of in camp, lent for the occasion by a cooperative madam in the Badlands section.

A sign on the bar, near the street entrance, read "Closed." Langrishe had expected objections to this decision, and he was right. Several customers were lined up, and one in particular was pounding on the wood and shouting for drinks in a shrill, carrying voice. Langrishe knew who that was before he caught sight of her. He walked over and said, indulgently, "You're making a great deal of fuss, Jane."

He had run across Calamity Jane a number of times around the camp—in fact, it was she who had helped him track down and arrange the loan of a piano. She sounded good-natured enough as she protested, "Aw, have a heart, will you, Jack? Open up the bar. How you expect us to last out the evening dry?"

"Well, now, Jane . . ." He took her elbow and turned her for a look at the crowd. "Doesn't it strike you these lads are noisy enough already? If I were to open the whiskey barrel, what shape do you suppose they would be in by the intermission? I doubt that my actors would be able to make themselves heard."

She thought that over, then shrugged with a grin. "Oh, all right, Jack. As a special favor. So go ahead—put on your show. And make it a good one!" She gave him a friendly slap on the shoulder that all but staggered him.

"We strive to please," Langrishe assured her.

Backstage, he found the usual state of ordered frenzy as last minute adjustments were made to makeup and costumes and to the improvised props. As usual he was quite pleased with the job by his stage manager, himself a seasoned veteran. Satisfied that all was ready, Langrishe called the company together for a few last words of encouragement.

"I know you're all a bit nervous," he said, running his glance across their faces. More than a few showed hints of pallor beneath the garish stage makeup. "And I'll not try to deceive you. I couldn't do that in any event, because most of you have worked places like this with me before. You know that, given an audience like the one you hear out front, nearly anything can happen. They might quiet right down, but if not, you mustn't let them disturb you. Simply treat this like any dress rehearsal. Remember to project your lines, and just ignore whatever happens out front. Play instead to your fellow actors—try to support one another. Don't forget, we're being paid to give a performance, and that's what I want you all to do. If there are enough people out there who actually want to see this play, they'll make the rest behave. If not—" Langrishe shrugged. "We've taken their money; it's up to them whether they enjoy themselves."

He paused to look at the gaudily painted faces of his troupe. "Are there any questions?"

There didn't appear to be. Nevertheless, he found his conscience was bothering him; he felt suddenly guilty at sending them out there not knowing of the threat he had felt best to keep to himself. He heard himself saying, "Oh! Just in case there *should* be any trouble . . ."

Bertie Clevenger, in the false curls and cap she wore for the part of Archibald Carlyle's old-maid sister, Cornelia, caught at something in his tone. As he hesitated, she prompted, "What sort of trouble, Jack?"

He drew back from giving the full explanation, afraid it might only demoralize them all. "Who knows?" he answered gruffly. "Probably nothing. But I do want it remembered that, in *any* emergency, I shall be counting on the gentlemen to offer the ladies of the company every possible assistance. I trust this is clear?"

There were nods, and Bruce Walker, who had just appeared with the cashbox and the evening's take, assured him gallantly, "They know they can always depend on us!"

"Fine." Langrishe consulted his watch again. Turning to the stage manager, he ordered briskly, "Get the footlights going, Harry." And to Fred Hamilton, who played the piano as well as doubling as a manservant, "Be ready to start the music. Curtain goes up five minutes after that. Right now I have to get into makeup." He dismissed them and started for one of the tiny dressing rooms to don

costume for his own role tonight—the aristocratic Lord
Mount Severn.

Ellen Dorsey had a question on the tip of her tongue
to ask Langrishe, but he seemed to pass over her deliberately, as if not seeing her at all. Yet in the next moment he
paused for a word with Claire Richards, who looked strikingly beautiful in the traveling costume Lady Isabel would
be wearing for her first-act arrival at her new home in East
Lynne.

Ellen was watching them, trying not to be hurt, when
she felt Bertie Clevenger's hand touch her arm and heard
the older woman saying, "Don't let that upset you. It was
done for our leading lady's benefit. I can tell: Jack is
simply trying to avoid any risk of her going into another
snit—tonight of all nights—about someone else getting
favored treatment. Believe me, *you* have no reason to be
jealous."

Ellen said quickly, "Oh, I'd never do that!"

In the half darkness backstage they heard the raucous
cheers and applause as a taper was applied to each of the
oil-lamp footlights, and a moment later, the piano tinkled
into life. Ellen felt herself go suddenly hollow. She had
been a part of enough audiences in her life to know the
signs of stage fright, but never had she witnessed a case as
bad as this one felt. Something made her ask Bertie, "The
last thing Mr. Langrishe said to us—about possible trouble:
What do you suppose he meant?"

"I just don't know," the older woman admitted slowly.
"I've never heard him talk that way before a performance."
Then she added, in a reassuring tone, "But, pshaw! He
probably didn't mean anything at all. Jack Langrishe himself is a perfect gentleman. I imagine that was just a way of
reminding the rest of the boys that he expects *them* to
be, as well. . . ."

The piano piece ended with a mighty tremolo, and
amid desultory applause Fred Hamilton came dashing back,
ready to join his wife onstage where as the family servants,
they would be discovered at curtain rise discussing Archibald
Carlyle's impending arrival at the ancestral halls with his

new bride. Ellen waited, with fingers crossed and breath
held, for *East Lynne* to commence.

Murdock and Renner were late arriving at the Bella
Union; shaving and cleaning up after a day on the trail had
taken longer than they expected. They found the play
already begun and, for all they could see, every seat
already taken. No one was selling tickets. Having let themselves in, they stood together at the rear of the auditorium
while they took in what was going on.

It was with some misgiving that Tom Murdock had
decided they should wear their guns tonight. The deep-
voiced man preferred not to depend on the threat of
gunplay to quell a brewing disturbance, but for this event
he felt that weapons were in order, since it was hard to say
what to expect of a Deadwood audience. This one, he now
saw, seemed at least willing to settle down and try to
follow the action onstage. If the setting, obviously meant
to be the parlor of a well-appointed dwelling, had an
improvised look about it, no one seemed to mind. There
was a general stirring among the humanity crammed onto
the benches or leaning from the boxes—a rumble of coughs
and shuffling of boots—but the voices of the actors seemed
able to rise above all such disturbances, carrying above
the heads of the audience to the rear of the little hall.

Suddenly, amid a flurry of welcomes, the newly married Carlyles burst upon the stage. When the men who
filled the hall saw the handsome leading lady, they began
to whistle and yell in a way that threatened to shake down
the roof. The play came to a dead halt, and Claire Richards beamed rather uncertainly at her reception.

Once the audience regained its composure, the performance resumed. Bertie Clevenger, as Archibald's sister,
stepped forward to make Isabel welcome in her new home.
But now, suddenly, Tom Murdock himself was paying no
attention to the play at all.

A line of men had just filed silently into the theater.
He counted seven, all of them armed, and he sensed
something sinister in the purposeful way they entered.
They looked over the audience and then, as though at a

signal, proceeded to split and fan out along the rear and sides of the hall. The one who seemed to be their leader took up a position at the very back, a short distance from where Renner and Murdock were standing.

Sensing that his friend was as suspicious as himself, Murdock asked under his breath, "Know any of them?"

"Just that one." Polk Renner nodded to the leader, a dish-faced fellow in a red shirt and brown pants, the lower part of his features all but lost in a massive black growth of whiskers. "He's Rupe Barrow. I saw him in action once, squaring off with some gent over a claim. He bluffed the other guy into backing away."

"Sounds like he'd be one of Johnny Varnes's friends."

"I've seen him hanging out with Creed Dunning. . . ."

Tom Murdock eyed the silent figure of Rupe Barrow, who stood with gun in holster and arms folded, hawkishly watching the play. All at once the stage-line owner had a bad feeling.

But nothing happened as the play continued. Toward the end of act one, Isabel was alone onstage with Archibald, and to the accompaniment of the piano in the pit, Claire Richards was picking up the strains of her song—"Then You'll Remember Me." It seemed to Murdock that the way she sang it didn't sound nearly as mellifluous as the few measures he had heard from Ellen Dorsey that evening in the hotel dining room, but then he supposed he could be prejudiced.

Not long after the leading lady ended her song, the curtain dropped with a bang on the floorboards, and amid boisterous applause Jack Langrishe stepped out before the footlights to thank the crowd and to introduce the newest member of the company. He outlined a completely fictitious biography, including successful seasons in San Francisco and Chicago, and then brought Ellen Dorsey out for her rendition of the biggest new hit of the year, a ballad entitled "I'll Take You Home Again, Kathleen."

Watching her as she stood in the glare of the oil lamps, waiting for quiet and for the piano to begin an introduction, Murdock's heart went out to her; she looked so fragile and alone. Though she appeared to be composed,

he could guess the terror she must be feeling. Yet after a
first shaky note or two, the voice that came from her
throat was a rich and self-assured contralto, sweet and full.
The constant undercurrent of sound in the hall began to
quiet, as even this rough crowd found itself forced to
listen to the plaintive melody and sentimental lyrics.

And then it came, just as Ellen drew breath at the
end of a line. A shout from Rupe Barrow suddenly rang
through the hall: *"That's enough!"*

As though she had not even heard, the woman on the
stage sang a few words more, but this time the man was
not going to be ignored. He strode forward to the head of
the center aisle that split the rows of benches, and his
heavy voice carried down the length of it, topping hers.

"I said that was enough!" His gun was in his hand,
and without warning he fired a shot over the heads of the
audience, into the closed front of the piano. The report
rocked the room; startled yells mingled with the jangling
of piano strings as the bullet struck. The elderly Fred
Hamilton almost fell off his stool at the keyboard, but with
an actor's quick reflexes he was on his feet in an instant,
keeping low and scuttling toward a door leading backstage.
Still onstage, Ellen Dorsey seemed to freeze where she
stood.

Renner grabbed his boss by an arm to hold him when
he showed signs of starting forward. "Tom, don't be a
fool!" he warned hoarsely, nodding to indicate the half-
dozen men who had entered the hall with Rupe Barrow;
they already were stepping forward, brandishing their weapons to back up their leader.

An angry reaction swept through the audience, but it
was instantly clear that the gunmen had them covered on
all sides, both the theatergoers on the floor and those in
the box seats. Barrow warned loudly, "Don't nobody inter-
fere with us—not if you know what's good for you!"

There were protests, but even though some of the
crowd was armed, no one wanted to be first to make a
move with those drawn guns threatening them. Now Jack
Langrishe strode out again on the stage. He made a mo-

tion to Ellen Dorsey, urging her off, but she seemed unable to move. At the footlights, Langrishe looked out over the audience and called down angrily to the ones who had taken control of his theater, "What is the meaning of this?"

"I think you heard!" Barrow retorted. "We're closing you down, Langrishe."

From the crowd a woman's voice—to Tom Murdock, it sounded like Calamity Jane's—shouted back at him, "You sonofabitch! What if we won't let you?"

In reply, a couple of Barrow's men fired shots at the ceiling, silencing further protest. A skylight smashed; dust and shards of broken glass rained down. The stink of burnt powder began to mingle with the smells of sweat and booze and burning oil.

Up on the stage, Ellen had both hands pressed to her face. To Murdock she looked like someone in the grip of shock, but now Bruce Walker came darting out from the wings to do what Langrishe had failed to accomplish. He got an arm around Ellen's waist and, gently turning her, led her off. Murdock couldn't fail to see the solicitous concern in the way the actor bent over her . . . or the trust with which she gave herself into his care. But it was hardly a time to think of being jealous.

Jack Langrishe seemed as self-controlled as ever. He showed no hint of fear as his fine actor's voice rang out with scorn. "I suppose all this is because I told that fellow Varnes I was not impressed by his threats."

"Did I mention any names?" Rupe Barrow retorted sharply. "I'm just telling you, unless you watch your step real careful, somebody is apt to get hurt. If you don't want *that*—"

Ellen's terror, and the name of Johnny Varnes, had decided Murdock—he had to take action, though he dared not draw his gun for fear of the safety of the theater patrons and performers. The distance between himself and Barrow was no more than a couple of steps. The man's back was turned, while everyone else's attention seemed riveted on the encounter between him and Langrishe. Murdock didn't hesitate.

Polk Renner must have guessed his intention. He reached out a hand to stop his boss, but Murdock shook it off, already striding forward.

He was almost within reach of Barrow when one of the leader's companions sang out sharply, "Rupe! *Behind you!*" Barrow turned quickly, dropping back a step. Murdock, caught in midstride without a chance to draw his weapon, found himself looking into the muzzle of a gun still smoking from the shot that drilled the front of the piano. Empty-handed, he could only stare at the gun and at the battered face behind it. The very room seemed to hold its breath.

Then with an effect like the crack of a whip, a voice said, *"Barrow!"*

It was a voice that demanded attention. Rupe's head was pulled around by it as every eye lifted to the box halfway down the right side of the hall. The person who sat alone in its shadowy interior had gone unnoticed up till then. Now he was on his feet, a giant figure who loomed in the curtained opening. He made no move to touch either of the guns strapped to his waist, but there was menace enough in the stillness of his figure, the tawny mane of hair tumbling to his shoulders, and the predatory beak of nose protruding above the silky, drooping mustache. The mere presence of Wild Bill Hickok—along with his reputation—could accomplish as much as a shout or a threat.

Rupe Barrow stood as though frozen. He scarcely seemed to notice when Murdock plucked the revolver from his fingers. Belatedly, he made a grab for it, then let a gust of air pass through his bearded lips as the gun's muzzle was rammed, hard, against his own ribs.

"This is where it stops!" Murdock told him sharply. "Don't do anything at all—and tell your friends the same. Tell them to stand still and to throw down their weapons!"

The bearded face within inches of Murdock's was all at once slick with perspiration. His speech came out in a hoarse bellow, relaying the order. "Don't argue with the sonofabitch!" Barrow cried, only half articulate. "He'll *kill* me!"

"No place here for the likes of you and me." A[r]
ed for the door to the familiar world on the oth[er]
he footlights.

k Renner followed without a word of comment.

One by one, the weapons fell to the floor. When a couple of Barrow's men were too slow about it, men from the audience leaped up and snatched the guns from their hands.

Murdock turned again to his prisoner, and his angry words were for Barrow alone. "What's it all about?" he demanded fiercely. "Has Johnny Varnes got some idea of taking over this camp by force? Was busting up this performance supposed to set the example—serve notice as to what it would cost, from now on, for anyone to do business in Deadwood?"

The man's eyes flickered; though he said nothing, for Murdock this movement was answer enough. "I thought it might be something like that. Well, you go tell Varnes that he bit off too much this time. The camp's not going to roll over and play dead for him—or for anyone else. I want you to tell him that. Now, get out!"

Still holding the captured gun, he gave Barrow a hard shove toward the street entrance. Polk Renner was there to grab the man and send him on. Suddenly, all through the hall, there were yells and catcalls and laughter as Barrow's men, stripped of their guns and their menace, received the same treatment. Within minutes, the Bella Union was clear of them.

Hands were slapping Murdock on the back, but he shook them off. He wanted to find the man really responsible for averting violence. Looking up, he saw that the box where Wild Bill Hickok had been sitting was empty—almost as though, having been forced to draw attention to himself, the man had decided not to stay around for any more. Odd behavior from one who was generally thought to search out notoriety and fame. . . .

Up on the stage, Jack Langrishe had his hands upraised, trying to make himself heard and restore order. "Resume your seats—please! Everyone! My apologies for this interruption. . . . No harm was done, except to the piano. As soon as the house is able to quiet down, we can continue our performance."

Tom Murdock was already on his way to the backstage door. He had never been behind the scenes at a theater, and no one invited him now; but there was something he had to know, and he wouldn't let anything stand in his way. He eased through the door, closing it behind him, and stood looking around at the confusing, alien locale, trying to orient himself.

To his surprise, Polk Renner was already there, earnestly talking with Bertie Clevenger, who stood with an arm around her daughter, Cindy. The little girl was wide-eyed but apparently not too disturbed. She had something of her mother's calm manner; it seemed impossible really to fluster either of them. Instead of Polk Renner comforting the widow after the ordeal, it looked to be the other way round, from the way she smiled and soothingly patted his rough and callused hand.

Murdock hurried over. "Sorry to interrupt," he said gruffly, "but what about Miss Dorsey? It was a bad time she went through, out there onstage."

"No need at all for you to be concerned, Mr. Murdock," the woman said.

He wondered just how she meant that and then guessed it himself: He wouldn't soon forget the picture of Bruce Walker with his arm protectively around Ellen's waist, or the way she had clung to him as he hurried her off the stage and to safety. . . . The Clevenger woman hardly needed to remind him, as he stood in this place with all its strange scents and sounds, that *he* was the outsider here, unneeded and unwanted.

But perhaps that wasn't what she meant, after all. She now smiled at him warmly and, lifting a forefinger, said, "Listen!"

From out in the hall came a burst of applause, and as it ended, the piano and then Ellen's sweet, clear voice began once more the song that had been interrupted.

"Do you hear that?" Bertie said. "She insisted on going right back out there even though she was every bit as shaken as the rest of us—and this her first performance, at that. Nobody can ever doubt that that girl is a real trouper after this! We should all be proud of her."

"I think so, too," was all Tom
and lamely at that.

Jack Langrishe appeared, smilin
tain amount of pallor beneath his
tightness of the flesh about his eyes b
had been under. He descended on
outstretched. "Delighted to see you a
as they shook hands. "Delighted! Tel
any idea what became of Hickok? He
have vanished—and I wanted to thank

"I don't think he wanted you to."

"Well, then you'll have to do for b
the younger man's arm vigorously. "We'r
in your debt."

Murdock tried to pass that off, bu
angle to the evening's events that he wan
"Is it true you were threatened by Johnny

"As a matter of fact, yes. I didn't take

"I take Varnes very seriously, Mr. I
been giving the stage line trouble; now i
thinks he's big enough to start cracking the
wood itself. Thanks to Hickok, he was stop
time he'll just know he's got to be better pr

They left off talking then to hear the
song. Most of the company—Murdock notic
Richards was not among them—had gathere
wings, listening. As the last clear note hung a
whole auditorium shook to boot stomping a
and Ellen came off looking stunned, obvious
such a reception.

Her friends surrounded her, but Bruce
there first with a hug and a kiss in front of th
Murdock had been hoping desperately for
speak to her, but he could see no way wi
people crowding around. Out front, the applaus
and now Jack Langrishe caught Ellen by a h
her out, flushed and happy, to take another bo

Murdock looked for his friend Polk Renne
moned him with a nod. "We better be going

roughly
he hea
side of
Po

Chapter 10

At the stage-line office, the open window beside George Faraday's desk let in the normal sounds of the wagon yard outside and the sprawling camp of Deadwood on an August afternoon, two weeks after the performance of *East Lynne*. The two seated men looked at each other in silence, the inconclusive words that had just been spoken hanging between them. Then Tom Murdock's chair creaked as he shifted position and laid a hand on the edge of the littered desk.

"You don't have to beat around the bush with me, George," he said quietly. "We've worked together a long time. So . . . out with it. What's bothering you?"

George Faraday shook his head and rubbed a palm across cheeks that were starting to sag with age. "I think you know what's bothering me. Three shipments lost in the past two weeks! When the devil is it going to stop?"

"I wish I could tell you. I can only say we've been doing our best."

"You must know I'm not blaming anyone," the older partner said tiredly. "It's a mean situation. You and Polk Renner and Ted Norton can't manage all the runs. And the company hasn't the money to hire all the guards we need."

Murdock said, "Even if we had the money, the guards just aren't there—not enough of the kind we would want, anyway. Men come to these hills looking to make themselves rich. They aren't eager to risk their skins protecting somebody else's gold. The sort of riffraff we might be able to pick up, I wouldn't hire. We could find ourselves paying them wages to rob the coaches they were supposed to guard."

"I know—I know."

Faraday was holding back. Murdock had known him long enough to recognize the signs. There was something he had made up his mind to say, something that his younger partner was not going to like hearing; it made Faraday reluctant to get it out. He took a breath and shrugged his shoulders to settle them.

"I told you, Tom, I'm not trying to lay any blame. I know what it's like for you in the field. But the longer this goes on, the more it hurts our reputation and the harder it makes the job for Mel Jenson, out there trying to drum up financing to keep us going. Something has got to be done about these holdups. I've reached a decision—"

"Yes?"

He seemed on the defensive about it. "I've got no choice. We aren't Wells Fargo. If we can't guarantee our gold shipments, then all I see to do for the time being is to stop sending them out. At least we've got a vault that no one's going to get into." He indicated the big metal box that occupied a corner of the office. "Starting today, I'm holding back all further shipments until the situation can be changed."

Tom Murdock stared at him. "That won't solve anything—only postpone it."

"That's the whole idea. To buy us time for finding a solution, without having what's left of our reputation damaged worse than it already is."

Again a stillness lay in the heated air of the office as the partners looked at each other across the desk. At last, Murdock said heavily, "All right, George. Scheduling shipments is your end of this operation. If your mind's made up, then it's for you to call the shots." No need to point out that the older man, by this decision, was laying the problem squarely on his partner's shoulders. Gold dust could pile up in the company vault for only a limited time before it became absolutely imperative that it be moved out. Tom Murdock was the man who was going to have to discover how to do that safely—and soon.

The discussion was interrupted as a pair of newcomers entered the office.

These were no strangers; they were, in fact, two of the more prominent citizens of Deadwood. One was the publisher and editor of the *Black Hills Pioneer*, a man named Merrick. The other was William Kuykendall, a dry goods merchant whom the camp universally addressed as "Judge," and who was said to be involved in a major project for building a flume that would insure Deadwood enough water to develop all its gold-mining potential. The presence of two such visitors at the stage line was enough to suggest important matters were afoot.

After an exchange of greetings, Murdock brought extra chairs to the desk. Kuykendall told him, "You're not too easy a man to get hold of."

"I'm out in the field a lot," he admitted.

"We know. So when somebody mentioned seeing you in camp this morning, we thought we had better try and track you down."

Murdock looked from one man to the other. "You have a problem?"

"I think we all have."

Kuykendall was a spare, tidy man with a quiet manner. With his neatly trimmed beard, he indeed had something of the appearance of a judge. Nobody really knew whether he was a judge or not, but in a place like Deadwood nobody much cared. Tom Murdock knew at least half a dozen men in the camp who were reputed to have been lawyers, though with no legal business to perform they had to exist by pick and shovel. But William Kuykendall certainly looked like a man of the law, and that was enough for Deadwood. He said now, indicating Murdock's partner, "Has George told you our idea about Hickok?"

"I'm afraid not. There were business details we needed to settle first. Since they seem to have been settled," he added dryly, with a glance at Faraday, "we can get on to other news. What do you have in mind?"

"We're concerned about the tough element in camp. . . . They used to be satisfied to hang out in the dives and pick fights among themselves, but ever since that near riot at the Langrishe theater opening two weeks ago, they're showing signs of getting out of hand. They go roaring through the camp in armed packs. They threaten storekeepers and businessmen, beat up anybody who fails to move out of their way."

Merrick put in, "They came into the *Pioneer* office yesterday. When my printer convinced them I was out, they got abusive—said to tell me if I wrote anything about them they didn't like, they'd be back to smash the press and scatter type in the mud of the street, like chickenfeed. I've been half expecting, ever since, to see them try it! I carry a gun, and I've armed my staff, but frankly we're no match for thugs like those."

"Deadwood's always been a tough town," Murdock said. "We've always had our share of muggings and robberies. But I have to agree that it seems like we're now dealing with an organized force—as if someone had found a way to channel that kind of violence for his own purposes."

"Tell me this, Murdock," the newspaperman said. "I was there that night at the Bella Union, covering the opening. When the trouble started and you took it on yourself to stop it, I distinctly heard you make such charges against that gambler, John Varnes. Did you know something? Or were you guessing?"

Tom Murdock shrugged. "I didn't have the kind of proof that would stand up in a courtroom. . . ."

"What courtroom?" retorted Kuykendall. "As long as the government won't allow Deadwood legal status, anything the camp wants done to keep order, we'll have to do ourselves."

"Which is the reason we're here," Merrick added. "A few of us are trying to organize. Can we count on you and George?"

Murdock looked at his partner, who said merely, "We're a part of the camp."

With a nod Murdock told the visitors, "We'll do whatever we can, naturally."

"Good!" Judge Kuykendall smoothed his beard as he chose his next words. "Right now we'd like your advice about this man Hickok. . . ."

One by one, the weapons fell to the floor. When a couple of Barrow's men were too slow about it, men from the audience leaped up and snatched the guns from their hands.

Murdock turned again to his prisoner, and his angry words were for Barrow alone. "What's it all about?" he demanded fiercely. "Has Johnny Varnes got some idea of taking over this camp by force? Was busting up this performance supposed to set the example—serve notice as to what it would cost, from now on, for anyone to do business in Deadwood?"

The man's eyes flickered; though he said nothing, for Murdock this movement was answer enough. "I thought it might be something like that. Well, you go tell Varnes that he bit off too much this time. The camp's not going to roll over and play dead for him—or for anyone else. I want you to tell him that. Now, get out!"

Still holding the captured gun, he gave Barrow a hard shove toward the street entrance. Polk Renner was there to grab the man and send him on. Suddenly, all through the hall, there were yells and catcalls and laughter as Barrow's men, stripped of their guns and their menace, received the same treatment. Within minutes, the Bella Union was clear of them.

Hands were slapping Murdock on the back, but he shook them off: He wanted to find the man really responsible for averting violence. Looking up, he saw that the box where Wild Bill Hickok had been sitting was empty—almost as though, having been forced to draw attention to himself, the man had decided not to stay around for any more. Odd behavior from one who was generally thought to search out notoriety and fame. . . .

Up on the stage, Jack Langrishe had his hands upraised, trying to make himself heard and restore order. "Resume your seats—please! Everyone! My apologies for this interruption. . . . No harm was done, except to the piano. As soon as the house is able to quiet down, we can continue our performance."

Tom Murdock was already on his way to the backstage door. He had never been behind the scenes at a theater, and no one invited him now; but there was something he had to know, and he wouldn't let anything stand in his way. He eased through the door, closing it behind him, and stood looking around at the confusing, alien locale, trying to orient himself.

To his surprise, Polk Renner was already there, earnestly talking with Bertie Clevenger, who stood with an arm around her daughter, Cindy. The little girl was wide-eyed but apparently not too disturbed. She had something of her mother's calm manner; it seemed impossible really to fluster either of them. Instead of Polk Renner comforting the widow after the ordeal, it looked to be the other way round, from the way she smiled and soothingly patted his rough and callused hand.

Murdock hurried over. "Sorry to interrupt," he said gruffly, "but what about Miss Dorsey? It was a bad time she went through, out there onstage."

"No need at all for you to be concerned, Mr. Murdock," the woman said.

He wondered just how she meant that and then guessed it himself: He wouldn't soon forget the picture of Bruce Walker with his arm protectively around Ellen's waist, or the way she had clung to him as he hurried her off the stage and to safety. . . . The Clevenger woman hardly needed to remind him, as he stood in this place with all its strange scents and sounds, that *he* was the outsider here, unneeded and unwanted.

But perhaps that wasn't what she meant, after all. She now smiled at him warmly and, lifting a forefinger, said, "Listen!"

From out in the hall came a burst of applause, and as it ended, the piano and then Ellen's sweet, clear voice began once more the song that had been interrupted.

"Do you hear that?" Bertie said. "She insisted on going right back out there even though she was every bit as shaken as the rest of us—and this her first performance, at that. Nobody can ever doubt that that girl is a real trouper after this! We should all be proud of her."

"I think so, too," was all Tom Murdock could say—and lamely at that.

Jack Langrishe appeared, smiling broadly; only a certain amount of pallor beneath his stage makeup and a tightness of the flesh about his eyes betrayed the strain he had been under. He descended on Murdock with hand outstretched. "Delighted to see you again," he exclaimed as they shook hands. "Delighted! Tell me, do you have any idea what became of Hickok? He suddenly seems to have vanished—and I wanted to thank him."

"I don't think he wanted you to."

"Well, then you'll have to do for both." He pumped the younger man's arm vigorously. "We're every one of us in your debt."

Murdock tried to pass that off, but there was one angle to the evening's events that he wanted to clear up. "Is it true you were threatened by Johnny Varnes?"

"As a matter of fact, yes. I didn't take it seriously."

"I take Varnes very seriously, Mr. Langrishe. He's been giving the stage line trouble; now it looks like he thinks he's big enough to start cracking the whip on Deadwood itself. Thanks to Hickok, he was stopped. But next time he'll just know he's got to be better prepared."

They left off talking then to hear the rest of Ellen's song. Most of the company—Murdock noticed that Claire Richards was not among them—had gathered here in the wings, listening. As the last clear note hung and faded, the whole auditorium shook to boot stomping and applause, and Ellen came off looking stunned, obviously pleased at such a reception.

Her friends surrounded her, but Bruce Walker was there first with a hug and a kiss in front of them all. Tom Murdock had been hoping desperately for a chance to speak to her, but he could see no way with her own people crowding around. Out front, the applause continued, and now Jack Langrishe caught Ellen by a hand and led her out, flushed and happy, to take another bow.

Murdock looked for his friend Polk Renner and summoned him with a nod. "We better be going," he said roughly. "No place here for the likes of you and me." And he headed for the door to the familiar world on the other side of the footlights.

Polk Renner followed without a word of comment.

Chapter 10

At the stage-line office, the open window beside George Faraday's desk let in the normal sounds of the wagon yard outside and the sprawling camp of Deadwood on an August afternoon, two weeks after the performance of *East Lynne*. The two seated men looked at each other in silence, the inconclusive words that had just been spoken hanging between them. Then Tom Murdock's chair creaked as he shifted position and laid a hand on the edge of the littered desk.

"You don't have to beat around the bush with me, George," he said quietly. "We've worked together a long time. So . . . out with it. What's bothering you?"

George Faraday shook his head and rubbed a palm across cheeks that were starting to sag with age. "I think you know what's bothering me. Three shipments lost in the past two weeks! When the devil is it going to stop?"

"I wish I could tell you. I can only say we've been doing our best."

"You must know I'm not blaming anyone," the older partner said tiredly. "It's a mean situation. You and Polk Renner and Ted Norton can't manage all the runs. And the company hasn't the money to hire all the guards we need."

Murdock said, "Even if we had the money, the guards just aren't there—not enough of the kind we would want, anyway. Men come to these hills looking to make themselves rich. They aren't eager to risk their skins protecting somebody else's gold. The sort of riffraff we might be able to pick up, I wouldn't hire. We could find ourselves paying them wages to rob the coaches they were supposed to guard."

"I know—I know."

Faraday was holding back. Murdock had known him long enough to recognize the signs. There was something he had made up his mind to say, something that his younger partner was not going to like hearing; it made Faraday reluctant to get it out. He took a breath and shrugged his shoulders to settle them.

"I told you, Tom, I'm not trying to lay any blame. I know what it's like for you in the field. But the longer this goes on, the more it hurts our reputation and the harder it makes the job for Mel Jenson, out there trying to drum up financing to keep us going. Something has got to be done about these holdups. I've reached a decision—"

"Yes?"

He seemed on the defensive about it. "I've got no choice. We aren't Wells Fargo. If we can't guarantee our gold shipments, then all I see to do for the time being is to stop sending them out. At least we've got a vault that no one's going to get into." He indicated the big metal box that occupied a corner of the office. "Starting today, I'm holding back all further shipments until the situation can be changed."

Tom Murdock stared at him. "That won't solve anything—only postpone it."

"That's the whole idea. To buy us time for finding a solution, without having what's left of our reputation damaged worse than it already is."

Again a stillness lay in the heated air of the office as the partners looked at each other across the desk. At last, Murdock said heavily, "All right, George. Scheduling shipments is your end of this operation. If your mind's made up, then it's for you to call the shots." No need to point out that the older man, by this decision, was laying the problem squarely on his partner's shoulders. Gold dust could pile up in the company vault for only a limited time before it became absolutely imperative that it be moved out. Tom Murdock was the man who was going to have to discover how to do that safely—and soon.

The discussion was interrupted as a pair of newcomers entered the office.

These were no strangers; they were, in fact, two of the more prominent citizens of Deadwood. One was the publisher and editor of the *Black Hills Pioneer,* a man named Merrick. The other was William Kuykendall, a dry goods merchant whom the camp universally addressed as "Judge," and who was said to be involved in a major project for building a flume that would insure Deadwood enough water to develop all its gold-mining potential. The presence of two such visitors at the stage line was enough to suggest important matters were afoot.

After an exchange of greetings, Murdock brought extra chairs to the desk. Kuykendall told him, "You're not too easy a man to get hold of."

"I'm out in the field a lot," he admitted.

"We know. So when somebody mentioned seeing you in camp this morning, we thought we had better try and track you down."

Murdock looked from one man to the other. "You have a problem?"

"I think we all have."

Kuykendall was a spare, tidy man with a quiet manner. With his neatly trimmed beard, he indeed had something of the appearance of a judge. Nobody really knew whether he was a judge or not, but in a place like Deadwood nobody much cared. Tom Murdock knew at least half a dozen men in the camp who were reputed to have been lawyers, though with no legal business to perform they had to exist by pick and shovel. But William Kuykendall certainly looked like a man of the law, and that was enough for Deadwood. He said now, indicating Murdock's partner, "Has George told you our idea about Hickok?"

"I'm afraid not. There were business details we needed to settle first. Since they seem to have been settled," he added dryly, with a glance at Faraday, "we can get on to other news. What do you have in mind?"

"We're concerned about the tough element in camp. . . . They used to be satisfied to hang out in the dives and pick fights among themselves, but ever since that near riot

at the Langrishe theater opening two weeks ago, they're
showing signs of getting out of hand. They go roaring
through the camp in armed packs. They threaten storekeepers and businessmen, beat up anybody who fails to
move out of their way."

Merrick put in, "They came into the *Pioneer* office
yesterday. When my printer convinced them I was out,
they got abusive—said to tell me if I wrote anything about
them they didn't like, they'd be back to smash the press
and scatter type in the mud of the street, like chickenfeed.
I've been half expecting, ever since, to see them try it! I
carry a gun, and I've armed my staff, but frankly we're no
match for thugs like those."

"Deadwood's always been a tough town," Murdock
said. "We've always had our share of muggings and
robberies. But I have to agree that it seems like we're now
dealing with an organized force—as if someone had found
a way to channel that kind of violence for his own purposes."

"Tell me this, Murdock," the newspaperman said. "I
was there that night at the Bella Union, covering the
opening. When the trouble started and you took it on
yourself to stop it, I distinctly heard you make such charges
against that gambler, John Varnes. Did you know something? Or were you guessing?"

Tom Murdock shrugged. "I didn't have the kind of
proof that would stand up in a courtroom. . . ."

"What courtroom?" retorted Kuykendall. "As long as
the government won't allow Deadwood legal status, anything the camp wants done to keep order, we'll have to do
ourselves."

"Which is the reason we're here," Merrick added. "A
few of us are trying to organize. Can we count on you and
George?"

Murdock looked at his partner, who said merely,
"We're a part of the camp."

With a nod Murdock told the visitors, "We'll do
whatever we can, naturally."

"Good!" Judge Kuykendall smoothed his beard as he
chose his next words. "Right now we'd like your advice
about this man Hickok. . . ."

Tom Murdock showed his surprise. "Hickok? What about him?"

"Isn't it obvious?" the newspaperman asked. "The man has been a legend for the past ten years or more. The other night in the Bella Union we saw how potent that legend is. It was touch and go. You risked your neck going against those men—for a minute it looked as though you'd be murdered right there in front of us. And then Hickok stood up and said just one word—and everything came to a stop! I never thought I'd see anything like it."

"How about it, Murdock?" Kuykendall wanted to know. "What do you think our chances are of putting that legend to work for us? Can he be persuaded to repeat the job he did in taming the wildness of those towns in Kansas, Hays City and Abilene? . . ."

Merrick added, "We realize, of course, that he's not here for his health—none of us are. We'd expect to make it worth his while."

But Tom Murdock said, "I can't speak for Hickok— I've never actually met him. I understand, though, that if there's money in it, he very well might be interested. In any event, it's certainly worth asking him."

"Will you join us? We'd like you to be there—after what you did at the theater opening, he can't help but know we mean business."

Murdock thought a moment, then replied, "Report has it he can generally be found at Mann and Nuttall's. Any reason not to go right now?"

The other two men looked at each other, nodded, then stood and followed Murdock from the office.

Things appeared slow at the No. 10 Saloon that day. Even the handful of regulars were missing, but the man they wanted to see was there. Hickok stood with an elbow on the edge of the bar, making conversation with the bald-headed proprietor. Judge Kuykendall returned Carl Mann's nod of greeting and then turned to the tall man with the tawny mustache and the shoulder-length mane of hair. "Mr. Hickok?"

The gunfighter returned his look without expression. "Yes?"

"If you can spare us a moment, we'd like to have a word with you. My name is—"

"I reckon I know your name, Judge. In fact, I recognize all three of you." He flicked a glance at Merrick. "The newspaperman, right?" The glance passed to Tom Murdock. "And I know *you*, of course."

"We're here as a delegation," Judge Kuykendall said.

"Representing who?"

The blunt question forced an admission. "To be honest," Kuykendall said, "mostly just ourselves. Although I do think we speak for the interests of the camp."

The tall man considered him for a long moment with that unwavering blue-gray stare. He lifted a shoulder then within the Prince Albert coat. "All right. Let's sit over here." He indicated a table, and picking up a bottle from the bar, he added, "Carl, give us some glasses."

The room was narrow, low-ceilinged, with the bar at one side and doors at front and rear. Hickok led them to a card table. Murdock noticed that he went around it and took a seat where the plank wall would be at his back and he had a clear view of both entrances. Murdock recognized this as a precaution that had probably become second nature for a man with his history as a gambler and gunfighter.

The others took places, and Hickok uncorked the bottle and proceeded to fill the shotglasses provided by Carl Mann. Intrigued by the chance to observe the famed gunfighter at close range, Murdock was a little puzzled to notice something studied yet unsure about his movements, especially the way he clinked the throat of the bottle against each glass just before he poured. This wasn't the uncertainty of somebody who had already drunk too much; on the contrary, Hickok was plainly cold sober.

Judge Kuykendall had begun to explain their mission. Murdock paid less attention to his words than to the tall man's reaction. As he listened, Hickok seemed suddenly to withdraw somewhere behind the pale surfaces of his eyes— and Murdock was somehow reminded of the way he had vanished, that other night, from his box at the Bella Union. He knew suddenly, even before the judge finished stating it, that Hickok was going to refuse their proposition. . . .

There was a pause and then a longer silence as they waited for an answer. His face a cold mask, Hickok finally said, "This all reminds me of a yarn I heard once— something about a smart monkey who fast-talked a cat into grabbing him some hot chestnuts out of a fire. You wouldn't be trying to turn me into a cat's paw, would you?"

The judge appeared shocked. "Certainly not! This is strictly a business proposition. We hope to make it worth your while. Name your price and let us see if we're able to meet it."

And Merrick, the newspaperman, pointed out, "It's no different at all from jobs you've taken on before—at Abilene, for instance."

"There's a big difference," the gunman retorted. "At Abilene, I was appointed to the job of marshal by the town council—and you're not that! You have no authority. You haven't even got a town!"

Kuykendall quickly said, "I can promise you, the responsible element here in Deadwood—"

"Will do what?" the tall man cut him off. "They'll sit back and watch, is what they'll do. I've seen it before. If I take your money and walk out on that street to preserve order, I'll be out there all alone, a target for every gun in camp. No, thank you, gentlemen," he said, with a shake of the head. "I'm a married man now, with a wife to consider. I don't think I'm interested in this."

He reached for the drink he had left standing in front of him, and Murdock saw how the backs of his fingers struck the glass, almost upsetting it. Hickok hesitated, frowning; then, watching what his hand was doing, he got the drink and raised it to his lips. Murdock was left staring, the thought shocking through him: *He has something wrong with his eyes!*

Hickok could not be very old—barely forty, if that. But a man's eyesight, Murdock supposed, could start to fail at even a younger age. For one whose legend and career had been built on cool courage in the face of danger—and, above all, on his marksmanship—this could be a desperate secret.

Merrick was demanding to know, "What can we say to change your mind?"

Abruptly Tom Murdock pushed back his chair, getting to his feet. "There's nothing we can say," he told the others shortly. "You won't change him. He's given his answer, so why not accept it? We'll have to solve our problem another way."

Judge Kuykendall, reluctant to admit failure, looked as though he wanted to make further argument, but at the implacable look of the gunman, he seemed to give it up. Rising, he said stiffly, "Thanks for your time, anyway, Hickok." And to the man behind the bar, "Carl, those drinks are on my tab."

The saloonkeeper nodded. There seemed nothing to add; they turned and walked out, leaving Hickok there at the table with his back against the wall.

Glancing back, Tom Murdock found the man's fierce stare pinned on him. It made him wonder if Wild Bill Hickok knew his secret had been discovered.

Chapter 11

Sid Krauss, the stage-line's yard manager, had a favorite listening post—a bench set under a window against the outside wall of Faraday's office where he sometimes worked at mending harness. He liked it because it allowed him to hear nearly anything that was said inside. This afternoon, as he was leaving, he paused briefly within earshot of this window while he dug out his smoke-blackened pipe and tobacco pouch and loaded up, tamping the shredded leaf into the bowl with a work-hardened thumb.

No sound came from within the office just now, however, except that of George Faraday shuffling papers. There being nothing to learn at the moment, Krauss stuffed the unsmoked pipe into a pocket and strode briskly out of the stage-line yard.

He crossed Deadwood Creek and, after walking along Main Street a couple of blocks, turned into an alley; this ended in a flight of steps leading up the steep north wall of the gulch. Scattered along the plateau at the top were cabins and other, more substantial homes belonging to Deadwood residents. Having reached the top step, Krauss heard from the gulch below him a busy murmur of sound— the whine of a sawmill, a pounding of hammers, the voices of men, and the grind of wheels passing through narrow alleys. Clouds of dust lined the streets, where only weeks before had been bottomless mud.

Krauss looked about with the guilty manner of one who hoped he was unobserved. Afterward he took a familiar path to the door of a house that on the outside appeared little better than a log hut, hardly different from

many of the others except that someone had had ambition
enough to put up curtains at the windows.

When Krauss knocked, there was no answer for a
moment. Then the door opened narrowly, and Pearl Varnes
looked out at him.

As usual, recognizing him, her eyes held no trace of
warmth, though Sid Krauss thought he detected a hint of a
smile. He quickly pulled off his hat and ran stubby fingers
through thinning, straw-colored hair. He could never seem
to speak to this woman. He doubted if she so much as
knew his name. To her, he was simply another of the men
who came to do business with her husband, and he as-
sumed she looked on him with disapproval and mistrust.
It made him shudder to imagine her opinion if she ever
found out the true nature of his business with her husband.
But he was in too deep now to back out, he reminded
himself.

Once, he thought, he might have been able to get out
of this racket. The very first time he came to this house he
had been desperate. After gambling away all the money
he had saved to set himself up in the hardware business,
Sid Krauss had borrowed more from the obliging Johnny
Varnes. But that money, too, he had gambled away, hoping to win back enough to repay his debt to Varnes and to
open the store. Luck seemed permanently to have for-
saken him. Faced with greater debts now than ever before,
Krauss had taken a job with the new Deadwood Stage
Line the previous spring, and though he had used most of
his wages to chip away at the amount he owed the gambling-
tent proprietor, he was still heavily in debt and in no
position to argue with Varnes when ordered to report all
important conversations between the stage-line partners.
Now Krauss wondered if he would ever be out of Varnes's
clutches. He also wondered if, when he was, he would be
able to stop visiting Varnes's house . . . and stop seeing
Pearl Varnes, even though she gave little sign of returning
or even recognizing his affection.

From the first time he had laid eyes on the wife of
Johnny Varnes, he had been smitten with her. Something
about her—something in her unhappiness and vulnerability,

haunting him and keeping her always on his mind—had brought him back again and again. In all these months he had never said a word to reveal that she—not the money Varnes deducted from his debt when he betrayed his employers or the occasional coins Varnes gave him to gamble with—was the real reason for his coming.

Now the woman said briefly, "He's here. Come in." She stepped aside as he entered, his hat in his hands. She closed the door and abruptly moved off into another part of the house, leaving him alone with her husband.

Johnny Varnes sat in a comfortable-looking chair near the window, a book open on his knee and a half-finished drink on the table at his elbow. There were other books stacked here and there on shelves around the crudely furnished room—Sid Krauss, who could barely sign his name, never failed to be impressed by the sight of them. He had once asked Varnes what it was he read, but the only name he recognized as ever having heard before was that of somebody named Milton. He wondered what the customers of Varnes's gambling tent in the gulch would have made of it, if they had guessed how the man used his spare moments.

Now Varnes closed his book on a finger, and the black eyes in his lean face looked at the caller impatiently. "Well?"

Krauss came nearer, so he could speak softly enough that the woman in the other room wouldn't hear. "Couple of things have come up, I thought you'd be wanting to know."

The gambler nodded impatiently.

"To begin with, there was some kind of showdown in the office this morning. They was fussing over how much they been losing lately, and finally Mr. Faraday, he up and lays it on the line. He told Murdock that, from today on, he was not gonna let any more gold shipments go out on the stages till they found some way of stopping 'em from being lost. Tom Murdock didn't sound too damn happy about it, but in the end he said Mr. Faraday could have it like he wanted. Until further notice, looks like they aim to let the dust pile up there in the office safe."

The other man's eyes narrowed in frowning speculation. "And what about the safe?"

"Oh, it's a good stout one—and I think you can bet they'll keep a guard posted. I doubt there's any way you could figure to get at it," Krauss said seriously.

Varnes considered, drumming lean fingers on the cover of the book. "This is a nuisance!" he declared finally. "It means I'll still have to make some kind of a play for those coaches from time to time—just to keep up an appearance that I don't have inside word they'll be travel-ing empty. A damn nuisance!" he hissed. Abruptly he changed the subject. "You said you had something else. . . ."

Sid Krauss nodded. "There was a couple of men dropped by the office. One was that fellow that runs the newspaper. The other has a funny-sounding name—they call him Judge."

"Kuykendall?"

"That's the one."

Johnny Varnes stared at his informant. "What the hell could *they* have wanted?" And then he listened, his expres-sion growing darker and more furious with every word of Krauss's hurried explanation.

"So!" he said finally. "They want to hire Wild Bill Hickok and turn him loose on this camp, do they?"

"Nothing came of it, though," Krauss said quickly. "They've already asked him. Tom Murdock went along, and about half an hour later he come back, and I heard him tell Mr. Faraday that Hickok said no, he wasn't interested."

"You're certain of this?"

"It's what Murdock said. And I thought you'd proba-bly want to know."

Johnny Varnes pursed his lips as he thought about this. Then he nodded curtly and tossed a couple of gold coins on the table in front of Krauss. "All right," he said, in a tone that told Sid Krauss he had been dismissed.

For several long minutes after the man had left, Varnes sat scowling at the dust specks drifting in the shaft of window light, working out the implications of the things his spy had reported. He stirred finally, reached for his drink, and discovered he had already finished the whiskey. He replaced the glass, then with an angry exclamation slapped the book down beside it and swung to his feet.

A man given to sudden bursts of energy, Varnes all at once was impatient to be in action. He took down his hat from the elk-horn rack on the wall. As he flung open the door, his wife entered from the hall, but he didn't wait to hear the question she asked him. Instead, he strode outside and took the path toward the steps leading down into Main Street.

Arriving at his place of business, Varnes scarcely noticed that it was, as usual at this hour, doing a brisk and satisfactory trade. Creed Dunning was talking to one of the lookouts who sat on a raised platform, shotgun across his lap. At the sight of his boss, Dunning started quickly toward him. Without interrupting his pace, Varnes indicated the office.

A mere cubicle, the office was partitioned from a rear corner of the tent and contained a table and chairs and a small box safe; a back door opened onto the alley. Varnes dropped his bony frame into a chair and placed his hat on the table; by then Creed Dunning had joined him. Assured of their privacy, Dunning leaned both hands on the table and began his news without preamble. "Johnny, there's the damnedest story going around. Somebody said Bill Hickok is fixing to run Deadwood!"

Varnes made an impatient gesture as he took a cigar from the case in his coat pocket. "I already know about that. He was asked to—by some of our more nervous citizens. He turned them down."

Dunning exclaimed, "By God, I hope you're right. A lot of the boys are really scared of Hickok . . . especially after he busted up Rupe Barrow's move at the Bella Union some weeks ago."

"Barrow was a fool!" Varnes snapped. "And so were the others we sent with him that night. They made themselves laughingstocks—and me one, too! But as for Hickok, I'm not convinced this thing is going to blow over, in spite of what he said today. Every man has his price. Kuykendall and the others will be coming back at him. They'll offer more—and sooner or later, he's apt to hear a deal that satisfies him."

Creed Dunning slowly nodded as he saw the sense of this. "What do you want me to do, Johnny?"

His boss gave him a long look. "Do?" he repeated, and then he came to a decision. "Nothing! This is no job for you . . . or for anyone who's known to be connected with me in any way. Instead, I want you to nose around quiet-like and find me someone that can be counted on to do what he's hired for, take his pay, and keep his damn mouth shut afterward."

Dunning, his eyes like slits, pursed his lips. Finally he said, "Yeah . . . I think I can do that. I got a man or two in mind. Leave this to me."

"I'd as soon you didn't waste any time over it."

Actually, it took less time than might have been expected. Some hours had passed, and shadows were beginning to pile up in the heart of the gulch; lamps were burning in the gambling tent, and the sound of the early evening trade was swelling loudly beyond its flimsy walls. Johnny Varnes, back at his desk after an early supper, had a ledger open in front of him when he heard the rapping of knuckles on the alley door. He recognized Creed Dunning's signal, but he nevertheless took out the gun he kept in the drawer of the table.

The door opened and Dunning entered, ushering a dark-haired man ahead of him—a man dressed in a black shirt and brown pants with a frame so slight that a strong wind might have threatened to blow him away. Yet despite his unimpressive size, an aura of wiry toughness did away with any question of the man's ability to survive. He looked at Varnes with eyes that didn't seem to work in unison, and Varnes felt a twinge of doubt. "Is this the man?"

"He's Jack McCall," Dunning answered. "I'll vouch for it he can do the job."

If he had not learned to have confidence in Dunning's opinions, Johnny Varnes might have questioned his choice. McCall did not strike Varnes as prime material at first glance; it might have been the slightly crossed eyes or his somewhat uneasy manner as he stood across the table. Varnes had seen him before around camp and had never been prompted to give him a second look. Then again, such unnoteworthy men were sometimes the best for certain purposes. . . . And he had Creed Dunning's endorsement.

With knowing shrewdness, he appraised the man and hit on a price. "How would you like to earn two hundred dollars, Jack?"

Not batting an eye, the fellow asked, "Who do I have to kill?"

Satisfied, Varnes nodded to the chair across from him, smiling crookedly. "Have a seat. We'll talk about it. . . ."

In front of the tent that he and his friends Steve and Charlie Utter had shared ever since their arrival in Deadwood a few weeks ago, the man they called Wild Bill sat in the sun writing a letter to his wife, Agnes Thatcher Hickok, of Cincinnati, Ohio, in his uneducated but sincere manner:

> Dead Wood black hills, Dacota
> My own darling wife Agnes. I have but a few moments left before this letter starts I never was as well In my life but you would laughf to see me now I just got in from Prospecting will go a way again to morrow I dont expect to hear from you but it is all the same I no my agnes and only live to love hur never mind Pet we will have a home yet then we will be so happy I am all most sure I will do well

He paused to dip his pen and sat for several long minutes frowning at the wall of the gulch in front of him. It bothered him greatly to lie, but he could not bring himself to admit to his wife that, after only a day or two, he had abandoned all pretense of hunting for gold and returned to his normal haunts and the gambling table. Agnes would be too disappointed, knowing he had lost his resolve and broken his promise to her.

Not that gambling had so far proved any more lucrative than prospecting. For the most part, his luck since hitting Deadwood had been rotten, and he was doing little more than break even. Although last night, at the No. 10, the cards had run somewhat better; maybe his luck was about to change. But last night also troubled him. He was thinking now about that fellow Jack McCall, who had elbowed his way into a place at the table.

Hickok had seen McCall around the camp and had found something repulsive about his slovenly manner and his face with the broken nose and eyes that didn't track properly. From the moment the man entered the game, Hickok had realized that McCall's whole attention had been riveted upon him. The man's stare never seemed to leave his face. McCall had played recklessly, heedlessly, and ended by losing everything he had. On an impulse of charity, Hickok had given him back enough of the money he'd lost to buy some supper. McCall had accepted the handout ill-naturedly and without a word of thanks.

Normally Hickok would have forgotten the incident. He didn't know why the malevolence he had sensed in Jack McCall continued to disturb him.

Passing a hand across his face, he pressed the lids of his closed eyes for a moment. Sometimes they didn't bother him too much; he could still put on exhibitions of shooting skill and marksmanship that nearly equaled his best performances in the past. But the pain and the blurring were more frequent now, and sometimes it frightened him. A shootist who could not depend on the sharpness of his eyesight was in serious trouble. So far he had kept his secret well guarded, or so he thought. Those men who came to him yesterday, with their offer of a job, obviously had known nothing about it—though toward the last he had wondered if one of them, the one from the stage company, might have guessed something. . . .

Well, he had got rid of them in any case. But there was no escaping the facts: This failing eyesight meant that sooner or later he would not be able to depend on the guns that had always been his mainstay and protection. Lately, he had found himself beset with dark premonitions

that would not go away. They led him now to take up
the pen again and finish his letter on a final, somber
note:

Agnes Darling, if such should be we never meet again,
while firing my last shot, I will gently breathe the name
of my wife—Agnes—and with wishes even for my enemies I will make the plunge and try to swim to the other
shore.

J B Hickok
Wild Bill

He addressed an envelope, folded and placed the
letter in it, and slipped both into a pocket of his coat.
Afterward, James Butler Hickok donned his flat-crowned
hat, carefully adjusted the hang of his clothing, and checking the high polish of his boots, started across town for his
daily afternoon occupation.

He found some half dozen of the regulars in Nuttall
and Mann's No. 10 Saloon. A workman had stacked lumber in one corner of the room and was in the process of
finishing off the rough interior walls, nailing pine boards
to the stringers. At one of the round card tables, a game
was already in progress. Carl Mann looked up from it and
hailed the newcomer, motioning him to come and sit in.
Hickok returned the greeting and stopped at the bar for
chips. But when he went over to join the players, he
suddenly hesitated, scowling.

A man of ingrained habit and constant precaution,
Wild Bill Hickok knew that the three men at the table—
friends, all of them—were well acquainted with how he
liked things to be. Yet his favorite place, the one that put
the wall at his back and gave him a view of both front and
rear entrances, was already taken, and from the grins on
the faces of the players, he knew it had been done
deliberately. He didn't find it a joking matter. "Charlie,"
he said sternly, "you're in my seat."

Charlie Rich met his look blandly. "Well, now, I
never seen your name on it, Bill."

"That place is always mine, and you know it."

"Today I got here first. Hell! You can't really think anybody here is fixing to sneak up on you."

"Course not!" Bald-headed Carl Mann, half owner of the saloon, continued, "We're all your friends, Bill. You keep on like this, you're gonna make us feel bad." He gave a kick to an empty stool, knocking it out from under the table. "Come on—relax! Sit down and look at some cards with us."

They were only teasing him, of course, but he made no effort to hide his anger as he let himself down onto the remaining stool. This placed Charlie Rich at his right and Carl Mann to his left; facing him across the round card table was Bill Massie, the old riverboat captain. Though Hickok had a good view of the street entrance, he was acutely aware that the other door, the one to the alley behind the saloon, was at his back, out of his line of vision. He didn't like the feeling it put between his shoulder-blades. . . .

The cards were gathered, cut, shuffled; the players anted, and the hands were dealt. The game continued.

Hickok began to lose from the start—irritatingly, in ways that made it clear to him he wasn't concentrating as he should. Thrown off by the constant reminder of a change in his unvarying routine, he lost a pot he ought to have easily taken. As he tossed in his cards, he tried again. "You've had your fun now, Charlie. So how about trading with me?"

Charlie Rich, stacking the chips he'd won, firmly shook his head. "I like this seat," he said complacently. "It's beginning to feel lucky."

Hickok set his jaw. He could not appear to beg; to do so would cause him to lose dignity over a thing his friends considered a mere eccentricity. He moved his shoulders within the Prince Albert coat to ease the knot of tension at his back, and settled himself as comfortably as he could on the hard, backless stool.

The lazy warmth of the August afternoon settled over the No. 10, and the stillness was broken only by desultory talk, by street sounds from beyond the open doorway, and by the pounding of the hammer nailing pine planks to the wall. A clean scent of new timber filled the room, mingling with the smells of whiskey and beer, of tobacco smoke and damp sawdust, which lay in drifts over the floorboards. Hickok waited for a change in his luck, but it failed to materialize. He had beaten Bill Massie the night before, but now the man in the riverboat captain's beaked cap was having a run that threatened to clean the gunfighter out. Finally Hickok had to call to the bartender for another fifteen dollars' worth of chips.

A newcomer entered from the street. Hickok glanced up but could not see him clearly against the blast of sunlight beyond the doorway. The man headed for the bar, and Hickok's attention went to the cards that were being dealt to him. He picked them up, one by one, and fitted them into his lean gambler's fingers. The ace of clubs . . . the eight of clubs—a possible flush? But, no: the spade eight—a messy pair. The jack of diamonds . . .

Then—the ace of spades! Two pairs; not much of a hand in itself, but it gave him a 693-to-1 chance of completing a full house on the draw. He eased the trapped breath from his lungs, letting nothing show in the hawkish set of his features. It could be . . . it just could be the change of luck he had been waiting for!

At the bar of the No. 10, it took Jack McCall a moment to realize his good fortune. When he did, he grabbed up his drink and swallowed it fast, his throat suddenly gone dry. But he scarcely tasted the whiskey. When he set the glass down again, his hand was trembling.

McCall had been ready to admit that the job he'd contracted to do for Johnny Varnes was beyond him. Nobody could openly confront a killing machine like Wild Bill Hickok . . . and the precautions the man took at every moment made any less obvious way of getting at him seem next to impossible, causing McCall a great deal of frustration. But last night, when he had got up from the gaming table, snatching up the coins Wild Bill had flung back at him, McCall had felt more than frustration, hating the gunfighter with a red fury for such blatant condescension.

The whole situation had seemed impossible . . . and now opportunity had been thrown into his lap! He had the sense to know that he would probably never see its like again.

He glanced around quickly. No one was paying him any attention—all too common a circumstance for Jack McCall. The barkeep was chatting amiably with a pair of customers; the workmen were busily fitting still another length of planking to the wall; the men at the table were engrossed in throwing poker chips into the pot. It was now or, probably, never. . . .

To get behind Hickok meant going directly past the table, and for a moment McCall's nerve nearly failed. But he steeled himself and went on, dreading at each step that the tawny eyes in the hawklike face would lift and settle on him . . . and read his intention as though it were written on his forehead. But Hickok seemed intent on the man who sat opposite him, absorbed in a challenge of wills over the cards both were holding. McCall walked past; he almost continued on to that alley door, to walk straight through it, but at the last instant his resolve gelled. Turning back, he looked at the broad shoulders of the man he meant to kill, at the tawny fall of hair ridged by the flat-brimmed hat.

He drew a step nearer. The .36-caliber Navy revolver slid from his waistbelt into his trembling hand.

At the table, Massie had shown his cards. Wild Bill Hickok said in disgust, "Well, I'll be damned! The old duffer—he beat me on the hand!"

McCall pointed his revolver. "Damn you!" he cried. "*Take that!*"

Following the explosion, muffled by the room, nothing at all seemed to happen. Through a burst of powder smoke McCall saw the head of the man in front of him jerk forward as the bullet struck; after that, Hickok and the others at the table remained utterly motionless for what felt like an endless time. Then, slowly, Hickok reeled and toppled to the floor on his back, the stool turning over with him. When he fell, the cards he had been holding were still clutched in his lifeless fingers.

The others around the table gaped at McCall and at the gun in his hand as though they failed to understand, just yet, what had happened. Wild Bill's killer was the first to recover. As he backed toward the alley door, which was now his escape route, his revolver menaced the room and he dared anyone to stop him, yelling, "All right! Come on, you sons of bitches!"

Suddenly in a panic, he aimed his gun at the bartender, lest the man should try to reach for the bar gun. The revolver's hammer fell; there was no report. Baffled, McCall swung the weapon at another target and tried again. Again—nothing. Dimly it occurred to him that the only good load in the cylinder had been the one that killed Hickok.

The others weren't waiting to learn that. Already there was a stampede for the street, leaving the murdered man lying in his blood. Jack McCall himself wanted nothing more than to be out of there. He turned, wrenched the alley door open, and plunged through it.

His deed had been all but unplanned—on the spur of the moment, with no consideration of what to do afterward. Not pausing, still carrying the useless weapon, he went at a run along the alley behind the buildings. Where it emptied into a side street, he looked frantically about and spied the rump of a horse tied before a building at the corner of Main Street. A horse was just what he needed now! On unsteady legs he headed for it. The animal was a bay, standing saddled and droop-headed before a hitching post. McCall freed the reins that held it there, found the stirrup, and flung himself astride. His jerk at the leathers made the horse rear as it backed into the street.

Suddenly, to his horror, Jack McCall felt the saddle sliding under him: Whoever this animal belonged to had left it with a loosened cinch. He fell heavily into dust that unnumbered hooves had pounded to the consistency of flour. Half blinded now by panic, he scrambled to his feet.

No time to try for another mount. . . . He turned and started scrambling up the slant of the street, with no other thought than to seek refuge at the huge tent belonging to

Johnny Varnes, the man who had hired him to do the murder. All around him now, dozens of excited voices seemed to be taking up the cry: "Wild Bill's shot! *Wild Bill's shot!*"

Jack McCall ran for his life.

Chapter 12

Tom Murdock had stepped into a dry goods store on Main Street to discuss an emergency shipment that the proprietor wanted brought in by stage rather than on one of the slow-moving bull trains. They were talking about weight and express rates when they heard the shouting start in the street. Curiosity drew them both to the doorway to see what was happening this time.

Murdock thought he glimpsed someone running up the gulch, the sunlight reflecting from something in one of his hands—possibly a pistol. Then the traffic swallowed him up. The excitement appeared to be farther down the hill, in the other direction, where a crowd was gathering. A man running past the store just then lifted a shout to someone in a wagon, of which Murdock caught only the words ". . . shooting at the No. 10!"

That was enough, for it reminded him that the No. 10 stood cheek by jowl with the Bella Union . . . where Ellen Dorsey would be! The thought of Ellen sent him instantly scrambling in that direction, cutting through street traffic to the opposite side.

The crowd was concentrated in front of the No. 10. Nearing, he saw that the door was closed and Carl Mann stood blocking it, shaking his head at anyone who wanted to enter. Murdock glimpsed Jack Langrishe and Bruce Walker next door, in the doorway of the theater, watching the excitement. Skirting the crowd, he approached them, asking, "What's going on?"

Above the noise he caught only a few words of Langrishe's answer: "a killing" and ". . . Hickok."

Murdock, drawing closer to Langrishe, echoed the name. "Wild Bill Hickok? Who has he killed?"

He saw the actor's bald head shake. "No, no. It was the other way around. I understand Hickok was playing cards, and someone walked up and shot him in the head."

Tom Murdock stared, scarcely able to believe what he'd heard. When Langrishe assured him it was true, he could only say, "None of your people are hurt?"

"What? Oh—not at all. The entire company was busy painting scenery. No one heard any shots or had a hint of trouble until all this hubbub began and we stepped out to investigate."

"I don't know—maybe you'd better stay inside and watch over the women. That's an angry crowd. . . ."

The door of the saloon opened, and Judge Kuykendall emerged, closing it after him. He was talking with Carl Mann as Murdock joined them to ask, "It's true? He's really dead?"

Their grim looks answered his question. Kuykendall ran a palm down over his neat spade beard and said, "Dead enough. According to Carl, here, a man named McCall shot him from behind, without any provocation, and then ran for it. Personally, I don't recognize the name."

"Me either—but I may have seen him running." Reminded of the one he had glimpsed earlier, gun in hand, Murdock peered in that direction and quickly exclaimed, "Looks like he didn't get far. . . ."

A clump of determined men was approaching down the center of the street, and they had a prisoner. He wore a battered, wide-brimmed hat, which hid his features as he was hurriedly propelled along, stumbling in the grip of his captors. When Murdock finally got a look at his face, he decided it was a man he had seen a time or two among the anonymous drifters who always hung around a camp like Deadwood. Just now, though, the face was slack-jawed and white with fear. Jack McCall's eyes, one of them decidedly crossed, darted wildly like those of a trapped animal hunting a way to escape.

One of those who held him captive sang out, "We got him! We got McCall! Where do we string him up?"

"How about that big tree behind the saloon?" a bystander called out.

Other voices eagerly picked up the suggestion, and the cry spreading, the crowd surged toward the prisoner, who suddenly began to buck and fight against the hands that held him. The hat fell from his head; his flailing boots began to kick up the powdery dust.

An angry shout somehow broke through: "No! No! Listen to me!" The threatened violence seemed to ebb as Judge Kuykendall strode forward, flinging up a hand. "Now, stop it!" he cried. "The lot of you! Nobody's going to be strung up—not without a hearing!"

The crowd didn't like that. Somebody cursed him, and another said loudly, "Why bother? We don't have to prove he's guilty. There was plenty saw it. *Him*, for one." He pointed at Carl Mann.

"Very well. Then let's get the witnesses together and have their testimony—according to the law."

"Law? Hell, everybody knows this is nothing but a coyote camp! There ain't no law here."

"Then it's high time we had some," Kuykendall shot back at him.

For all his slightness of build, there was something in the judge's erect bearing and level sureness of manner that commanded attention. They were listening in spite of themselves. Still, to Tom Murdock the decision appeared very much a matter of touch and go until Merrick, the newspaperman, hastened to throw his weight into the argument. "The judge here is right! Don't you see? Here's a chance to show the world that Deadwood means business."

Next thing Murdock knew, he himself was calling out. "Listen! This isn't some claim jumper that's been murdered. It's Wild Bill Hickok—one of the most famous men in the country. Everyone is going to be watching to see what we do about it. We may never have an opportunity like this again!"

The crowd grew still, though it had grown so large by now that it almost filled the street in front of the saloon.

Murdock thought he could almost smell the fear emanating from Jack McCall as the prisoner waited to see which way their decision would go. If they really wanted to hang him, there was not much anyone could do to stop them. But the first frenzy of lynching fever seemed to have cooled, though now one of those who held McCall demanded skeptically, "And where do you gents figure to have this trial? If you aim to hold court, you got to have a hall or something, ain't you?"

"Well, gentlemen . . ." It was Jack Langrishe, who unexpectedly had moved up beside Murdock and the judge. "If you're actually serious, I may have a solution for that. There's the theater, right next door here. I'll be more than pleased to donate it for your use. It seems the very least I can do—anyone who was present for our first night knows that if not for Mr. Hickok, we might never have managed to open at all. So just tell me when you need it."

"You're more than generous," Judge Kuykendall said. "We'll be pleased to accept. That is," and he looked pointedly at the crowd, "if everyone's in agreement. . . ."

A few still wanted to protest, but the big fellow holding the prisoner—apparently a self-appointed spokesman—drowned them out. "Oh, what the hell. Let's make it legal. Maybe do him good to stew awhile before we hang him—he'll end up just as dead, after all."

"Then it's settled," Judge Kuykendall stated, and it seemed that it was. "We'll have to elect officers of the court and draw up a jury panel. By tomorrow morning we should be organized and able to proceed."

"And what about McCall, meantime?" someone demanded. "Maybe you ain't noticed, but we don't have no jail, either."

"I know an empty building down at the foot of the street that should hold him," a big miner said. "We'll throw him in there and padlock the door . . . and post a guard."

There was no more discussion. The prisoner had been led away and the crowd was beginning to disperse when Charlie Utter arrived.

A lean and intent fellow clad in buckskins, Colorado

Charlie was an old friend of Hickok's. Having just learned the news, he was in a dark and violent mood. He had brought the camp barber with him, a mustachioed and stocky individual called—for no sound reason—Doc Peirce, who served Deadwood as an undertaker. Carl Mann, still guarding the door of the No. 10, unlocked it, and Tom Murdock followed the others inside.

Everything had been left just as it was—chips and cards scattered, a couple of stools overturned. The dead man lay on the floor; somebody had put a blanket over him. Charlie Utter drew it back, and they stared in silence at the giant of a man who now lay motionless on his back with eyes closed, looking almost as though in sleep. Murdock thought he could still catch, faintly, a tang of burnt powder hanging in the close, still air.

Doc Peirce cleared his throat, an explosive sound in the quiet. "Makes a real pretty corpse," he said with professional approval. "Must of been a small caliber pistol, maybe a .36—you can see that the bullet never even chewed his face up much when it come out. I can fix him up to look just fine."

"Do a good job, Doc," Charlie Utter said roughly. "I'm having a box made. I want you to put his guns in with him. I'll take him to our tent when you're done and bury him from there tomorrow."

They were talking of such details when Carl Mann beckoned to Murdock. From a pocket of his vest he took playing cards, spreading them out on the bar. "These are what he was holding when he got it—I took them out of his hand."

Murdock looked at the pairs of black eights and aces. "Nothing there to brag about."

"Pretty damned unlucky for Bill Hickok. Holding them, he lost the pot and then his life." Gathering up the red-backed cards, he said, "But I'm thinking I should have them framed. . . ."

In the Bella Union, the smell of freshly painted canvas was strong. Members of the theater company, dressed in old clothes for the day's work, stood about in little groups, their own business forgotten as they discussed in hushed voices the tragedy that had struck so very close to them.

Ellen Dorsey caught sight of Murdock the moment he entered and without hesitation came to meet him. Unusually subdued, she looked a trifle pale in the glow from the skylights overhead. When Murdock took her hands, they felt cold. "Are you all right?" he demanded, his deep voice displaying his concern.

"Of course," she said quickly. "But—it's so horrible to think of a *murder*—right next door, and none of us even knew! Tell me—was it really Mr. Hickok?"

"Yes."

"That makes it worse!" she exclaimed. "Somebody I knew—at least I felt as if I did." She went on, staring into space, "I met him one day, out in front of the theater. There was a—a man who tried to bother me, and Mr. Hickok simply walked up and sent him packing. We talked for a while about what it's like to be on the stage. He was such a strange person." She turned toward Murdock, her voice hushed but compelling. "It may be I'm only imagining it, Tom, but that day there was something about him—something about the look in his eyes, almost as though he knew even then that he didn't have very long. . . ."

At another time Tom Murdock might have agreed that it was probably imagination; today, he was not so sure. Then he realized that he still had both of the woman's hands in his, and self-consciously he let them go. He was trying to think of something reassuring to say when they were interrupted.

Bruce Walker had come in from the street. "Ah—Murdock!" he sang out. He slipped an arm comfortably around Ellen's waist, in a most natural way—almost as though unaware that he did it. "Have you learned any more about this Jack McCall? Any reason been given for what he did?"

Murdock tried not to see the hand curved around Ellen's supple waist. "Not that I've heard. But the man he shot was Wild Bill Hickok, which could have been all the reason he needed. Perhaps we'll learn something tomorrow morning."

"Perhaps we will."

And Murdock was left wishing he could really dislike this man who evidently felt no inhibitions about taking Ellen Dorsey into a casual embrace. It would be a relief, he thought, to hate Bruce Walker. Too bad that he had to find the man so completely likable. . . .

The Bella Union had never seen a drama like the one that was in the process of being staged as Murdock arrived next morning just after nine o'clock. At an organization meeting, held when the theater was cleared after the last evening's performance, a judge had been chosen—that it would be Kuykendall had been a foregone conclusion—as well as a clerk and a sheriff, to be put in charge of the prisoner. A panel of prospective jurymen had been drawn up from the three largest camps on the creek, and attorneys for the prosecution and defense were found among the town's lawyers, who had had no other legal business since their arrival.

Entering the theater now, Tom Murdock found the trial already underway. The room was crowded, but he found a seat toward the back. Kuykendall's bench was a yellow-pine table placed at the front of the hall, a chair beside it for a witness stand. A double row of chairs served as the jury box. The prisoner, under guard, sat up on the stage in full view of the audience. Murdock suspected that the show of disdain McCall put on covered his real feelings of terror. He had pleaded not guilty, and now names were being drawn from a hat for selection of a jury.

It was turning out to be a lengthy process, finding twelve men acceptable to both sides. When finally they were sworn in and seated, Tom Murdock had a strong initial feeling that all was not well. Most of them were jackbooted miners who probably resented the time lost from working their claims. Among them, however, he spotted three men who looked like the very element of Deadwood's floating population that Wild Bill Hickok, only two days ago, had been asked to help bring under control. Up to now, Jack McCall's conviction for murder seemed inevitable; as testimony began, Murdock tried to continue believing it.

The first witnesses established the place, time, and circumstances of Hickok's death. Charlie Rich blamed himself bitterly for having teased his friend by refusing to yield up Hickok's usual place with his back to the wall—a joke that had tragically backfired. No one remembered having even noticed McCall before the shot and his shout of "Damn you, take that!" and seeing the gun in his hand and Hickok starting to topple to the floor.

Bill Massie, the old steamboat captain, held up a bandaged arm for the room to see. "The first I knew, I heard a gun go off, and suddenly my wrist went numb. Later I realized I must have been hit by the same bullet, but *after* it killed Wild Bill. We hunted all over the room, but we never found the bullet, so I guess I still got it in here!"

The testimony was clear and unanimous in that McCall had deliberately and without warning or provocation been the cause of Hickok's death. The defense brought on a few witnesses who testified to McCall's upright character and to what they termed the "bad reputation" of the deceased. Called on then to speak in his own behalf, the defendant rose and came down the steps from the stage with an arrogant show of defiance.

"I only got one thing to say," he told the crowd in a loud voice. "Sure, I killed him—and he knew why! Wild Bill Hickok was a shootist and a murderer. No ordinary gent could hope to stand up to him. Back in Abilene, Kansas, he killed my brother. What's more, he promised to do *me* in if I ever crossed his path." He paused as the crowd gasped and whispered to one another. "I was just making certain he wouldn't get to me. I watched for my chance, and I killed him—and I'd do it again to save my own skin!" He strutted back to his place on the stage, leaving the court to absorb this bit of melodramatics.

The rap of the beer mug Kuykendall had been using for a gavel adjourned the court. The jury withdrew to consider its verdict; the prisoner was returned to his makeshift jail cell. As the crowd poured out from the hall, loud in discussion, Tom Murdock was overtaken by his partner, George Faraday, and by Polk Renner, who was fairly seething over the statement they had heard from Jack McCall.

"That ignorant sonofabitch! Who did he think would believe any part of a story like that?"

Faraday agreed. "Showing contempt for a jury's intelligence is surely the quickest way to turn them against you. What do you say, Tom?"

"According to what Carl Mann told me, evening before last, McCall sat in a game with Hickok, and Bill cleaned him out—and then gave the scoundrel back enough to buy something to eat! That doesn't fit with anything in his yarn about a brother, or about Bill threatening him." He hesitated. "On the other hand, it would be a poor gamble to bet on which side a jury is going to come down."

Renner stared at him. "You don't really think there's a chance in hell they'd turn him *loose*, do you? Why, it would be like giving the go-ahead for every crook in camp to do any damn thing he wanted here in Deadwood—from the big fish like Johnny Varnes on down! If they don't give that back shooter what he has coming—"

Polk Renner was working himself into a lather with anger; a vein was beginning to stand out in his forehead. Murdock placed a hand on his arm. "No point getting excited, Polk. We don't know what's going to happen. Go have a beer and cool off. You may have time for more than a short one. This could take longer than any of us think. . . ."

Chapter 13

Tom Murdock's prediction about the length of the jury's deliberation turned out to be right. An hour passed, then another, and still the waiting camp got no word from the hotel room where the twelve-man jury had been moved, under guard, for what many had expected to be a quick verdict. And as time drew out, Murdock suspected it could mean only one thing: trouble.

He stayed close, working with Sid Krauss on an inventory of the stage line's equipment and then examined the well-used harness and collars to determine what items absolutely needed to be replaced from the company's limited funds and what could be made to serve for a few months longer. It was a dull job, especially working with the taciturn and bad-tempered yard manager, but it needed doing, and it was a way to pass the time.

Within sight of the stage-line office, a steady stream of visitors had begun to collect around the canvas tent where Charlie Utter had placed his friend Hickok on view in a pine box covered with cheap black cloth. When Murdock went over to pay his respects, he found Colorado Charlie fuming over something that had happened earlier.

"Would you believe it?" Hickok's friend said in stout indignation, spitting into the dust. "That damned Calamity was in here, drunk as usual, crying and carrying on about her and Bill—how he'd been her man, and she promised to stay true to him forever. Why, hell! Bill thought too well of himself. Last thing he'd have done was give that trollop the time of day! But now she's gone and cooked up a way to put herself in the center of things, and I guess she means to stick to it. She was carrying on about cutting herself off a piece of his hair for a keepsake when I got disgusted and threw her out. . . ."

At three o'clock, a funeral cortege left the tent for the nearby cemetery, which so far held only a scattered handful of graves. A man called Preacher Smith, who tramped the gulches and delivered his sermons in the street for lack of a pulpit, rode next to Charlie Utter on the seat of the lead wagon. The rig contained the coffin and a wooden headboard—with Hickok's name misspelled—that Charlie himself had carved out and painted.

Tom Murdock watched them start out, followed by a motley procession that looked as though it contained half the population of Deadwood. Very few of these people were actually mourners; most were trailing along solely out of curiosity. Murdock preferred not to add to their number. Instead, realizing he had forgotten to eat anything since breakfast, he cleaned up and walked across town to the Grand Central to see if the dining room was still serving.

The first thing he saw as he entered the nearly empty room was Ellen Dorsey, seated alone at a table near a front window. She had her head turned away, looking out into the street, and her shoulders were slumped in discouragement or some other dark emotion.

Murdock was reluctant to intrude on her privacy, but his concern for her overrode his hesitation. He walked over and hesitantly spoke her name. She looked up as though startled but then managed a smile of what seemed genuine friendliness. When she invited him to sit with her, Murdock accepted a trifle awkwardly, explaining that he meant to order a meal. "Go right ahead," she said. "I'm not hungry, myself, but it's pleasant to talk."

The waiter came, and Murdock ordered beef stew. Afterward, anxiously studying Ellen, he said, "You were looking mighty solemn when I walked up just now. Are you still upset about the killing?"

Her brow clouded. "I suppose—I don't know. I think it's more than that."

"Anything that somebody else could help with?"

She shook her head but then suddenly let her worries

spill out. "It's just this place, I'm afraid—some of the things I can see, sitting here at this window. The dirt, the trash, the ugly buildings that are already half falling apart . . . I told you that when I first saw the Black Hills, I thought it was the most beautiful country I'd ever seen. But until I reached Deadwood, I had no real idea what was being done to it—the way they've torn up the earth and ruined the streams and stripped off the timber—"

"I know," he told her soberly. "To the Sioux Indian this was a sacred land—the Paha Sapa. And now he has to watch it be destroyed. No wonder he hates the white man. But I'm afraid it's an old story with us—called greed."

"It makes me feel ashamed to be a part of it."

He shook his head. "You've done nothing . . . no reason at all to blame yourself. About me, though, I'm not so sure."

"What do you mean?"

He tried to explain. "It's true I wasn't after gold. I haven't been tearing up the land or chopping down the forests. But I've built stage roads. And week after week I've helped bring in the men who *are* doing the damage—and all for profit, for my partners and me. No, I figure I've got a lot to make amends for."

Murdock's dinner was served just then, bringing a welcome interruption. When they were alone again, he glanced at the woman and found her studying him with serious intentness. "And how might you 'make amends,' as you call it?" she said slowly.

"That's something I haven't thought out yet," he admitted. "But everything passes. Gold fields play out; men make their fortunes or go broke. Either way, eventually they leave. Then's the time for the men who *don't* leave—the ones who decide they've got to stick around—to rearrange things. Of course, we can't put everything back just the way it was, but we can try to save what's left."

"I wonder how many others feel about it the way you do."

"Who knows? At least a few, though. Maybe enough . . ." He never felt comfortable talking about himself, and

abruptly he changed the subject. "Will there be a performance tonight?"

The question seemed to jar Ellen from her train of
thought. "Oh . . . yes, there's supposed to be. We're
doing *The Ticket of Leave Man* this week. Have you seen
it?"

"Yes, of course—the first night. You were just great."

"I think maybe I *am* getting a little better," she
conceded. "I seem to be learning, and from some very
good people. About tonight, though—Mr. Langrishe has
been to the judge and explained that if there isn't a
verdict, we're going to need the theater back. I understand they've agreed to move court to the saloon next
door, and when the jury brings in its verdict, the judge
will hear it there. That reminds me—" She consulted the
tiny gold watch she wore pinned to her shirtwaist. "Oh,
my! I've got to be going. Mr. Langrishe wants to change
the blocking for a couple of the scenes, and if I don't
hurry, I'll be late."

She rose quickly, and Tom Murdock got up, too. But
Ellen seemed reluctant to leave. She exclaimed, with
obvious earnestness, "I wish I didn't have to rush off this
way. . . . I really enjoyed our talk."

"I did, too," he said. Clearly, they both meant it.

Time passed slowly that day. It was nine o'clock—the
sky above the gulch not yet dark but turning to steel
above the ridges—when word spread that Jack McCall's
jury was on its way to report its verdict. When Tom
Murdock heard the news, he hurried across town and met
Polk Renner in the deepening shadows of Main Street.

Renner sounded like a man in shock. "Tom, you just
missed it. They let him *go*! I never believed you when you
tried to say it could happen. How the hell did you know?"

"I didn't," Murdock said curtly. "But I didn't like the
looks of that jury, either. A good number of them seemed
to be the kind that would use hard cash or threats or
anything else to make the rest vote McCall not guilty."

Polk Renner swore. "You should've seen McCall when
they brought him in and set him down—he was so scared

he damn near shook the chair to pieces. Then Kuykendall read the verdict, and by damn, I expected all hell to bust loose! But I guess we all was too stunned to do anything about it. Kuykendall let the jury know what he thought of them, but by then it was too late. McCall walked out of there a free man. He'll be a hero now to them that didn't like Wild Bill making them pull in their horns!"

Tom Murdock nodded a few times, visibly let down after these hours of waiting. "Oh, they'll make it tough for the rest of us, all right," he admitted bleakly. But then he added, "We'll just have to be tougher!"

Three days after Jack McCall's trial, as Murdock was talking to Sid Krauss about an injured horse, George Faraday called him into the stage-line office. The senior partner had a letter, just arrived from Custer City by way of Charlie Utter's express. He handed it over without a word, and Tom Murdock sat on a corner of the desk to read this latest report from the third partner, Mel Jenson.

When he had finished, he frowned, thoughtfully tapping the paper against a thumbnail. Slowly he said, "Wells Fargo . . ."

Faraday had been pacing, waiting impatiently while his partner read the letter. He said now, "We've known they'd be coming in here—they follow every big strike. We also know why they've held off from this one as long as they did."

"Of course," Murdock agreed. "As long as Deadwood's sitting on an Indian reservation, there'll be no mail contracts to be had from the government; that's always been Wells Fargo's main business. Still, with more and more gold being produced and shipped, they were bound to want in sooner or later."

"The question is, are they going to want to deal with us as carriers—and put their express boxes and guards on our stages—or will they bring in new equipment of their own? If they do that, of course, they can soon have us out of business. We haven't a chance of lasting against that kind of competition." Faraday indicated the letter in his partner's hand. "But Mel seems to think he can make a deal. Unless, of course . . ."

After a moment, Murdock said, "You don't even have to finish. You mean, unless they look over our records for holdups—and find out that, right now, we've got a vault crammed with dust we haven't dared even to send out. Why should they waste time on such an outfit? They'll most likely give us one choice: sell out to them at their price, or be put out of business—by a company that is big enough to handle the situation."

"Maybe," the senior partner suggested, without real conviction, "when they understand what we've been fighting, with such limited resources . . ."

"Excuses don't matter . . . only results."

"You sound as if you think we're already licked."

"*No!*" Tom Murdock swung restlessly to his feet, tossing the letter onto the desk. "Not after all the sweat we've put into this stage line! Obviously, we don't have a lot of time, but there *has* to be a way to use it. And this one's for *my* department," he added gruffly.

After a minute had passed, he said, "George, suppose we try to trick whoever is doing this into thinking the gold is being shipped in one wagon—actually load the gold onto that wagon—and then, on the trail, switch it to a coach that's supposed to be carrying just passengers. We could surround the decoy wagon with guards and make it look very convincing. The robbers would be aiming to ambush the wagon and wouldn't even think twice about the stagecoach going by on its regular run, and the coach would carry the gold right under their noses all the way to Custer City!"

"I think you've got it, Tom!" Faraday exclaimed. "Wells Fargo couldn't do better. Now . . . when should this scheme be carried out?"

"Why not do it late next week when the southbound coach is scheduled to make the run? That way we'd have time to prepare."

"Sounds fine to me. I'll let you make the arrangements, Tom, but if I can help in any way—"

"Don't worry, George. I'll handle it. . . . I'll let it be

known a shipment of gold is going out, and we'll see if someone takes the bait. Perhaps then we'll be done with these holdups once and for all."

As the two men shook hands, Sid Krauss, crouched outside the stage-line office window, knocked the ashes from his pipe, pocketed it, and headed for the hill that led to Johnny Varnes . . . and Pearl.

Murdock knew his plan would not be easy to execute. The man he wanted to talk to just now was Polk Renner—a solid, steady-thinking fellow who knew the situation as thoroughly as Murdock did himself. He headed for Main Street, hoping to find him, but instead he was hailed by a pair of men who came hurrying to him across the crooked, dusty street.

Jacob Studer and Herb Glennon were miners, partners in one of the best-producing placer claims in the gulch. The stage line had carried several shipments of dust for them, losing only one to road agents, but today the pair had a good number of leather pouches lying in the company safe, backed up and going nowhere because of George Faraday's prohibition against sending out any more shipments. The two men had something they wanted to discuss, and Murdock knew he had better take the time to hear it. Accordingly, he agreed to the suggestion that they step into one of the saloons for a drink. "I could use a beer, I guess."

They bought their drinks and carried them to a corner table, where they could talk somewhat privately. Murdock sampled his beer, then said without preliminaries, "What's on your mind?"

"Plenty!" Studer, bald and heavily mustachioed, was a ruddy-faced German whose shoulders were bowed and hands permanently warped by years of handling the tools of his occupation. "What's this talk we hear about Wells Fargo coming in?"

Murdock slowly set down his glass and exclaimed, "How does news get around this camp, anyway?"

"I guess it came from one of Charlie Utter's express

riders. He picked up some talk about it, last time he was in Cheyenne."

"I see. . . ."

Glennon had a less patient temperament than his partner, and now he demanded, "Well, is it a fact?"

"A strong possibility, at least," Murdock admitted. "I'd say it was overdue, knowing how Wells Fargo works."

"Herb and I are wondering," Studer told him, "what this will do to you and your stage line? How are you going to compete? Hell, they could push you right off the roads!"

Murdock had to smile, though a trifle grimly. "There's a bright side to everything. After all, for you and the other boys it could be a better deal all the way around. Wells Fargo can insure your dust for you, and if they don't deliver, it's their loss. Dealing with us, you're just out of luck if we lose a shipment. You've all been mighty patient," he added. "Longer than we had any right to ask."

Glennon waved that aside. "For God's sake! You and the men who work for you have risked your hides getting our gold through! Now that it looks like you're in trouble, it don't seem right if we can't do something in return."

"If there was just some way we could help," Studer said. "I got a gun, and I can use it if I have to. But a gun won't do any good competing against an outfit like Wells Fargo."

Tom Murdock looked at these men, at the earnestness in their faces, and another idea came to him: Why not hire gunmen to ride in the coach in place of paying passengers?

"Just supposing guns *would* give us some help . . ." he said, "you know any others in the camp that might feel the same as you?"

"More than you might guess, Murdock," Herb Glennon answered promptly. "Take it from me, you're a highly respected man here in Deadwood. A lot of the boys realize what you've been doing for them, and they appreciate it. If there's help some of us can give you, tell us what you need and I reckon we can find the hands to do it."

"This is only a notion. I'm not even sure it would be worth the risk."

"Try it on us. We'll tell you what we think. . . ."

Just then a trio of newcomers entered noisily from the street. Murdock, facing the open door, glanced up and suddenly stiffened. He heard an exclamation in German from Jacob Studer as both men, following his glance, saw Jack McCall swaggering toward the bar.

Murdock had not seen McCall since the trial, and now he saw a changed man. The killer's whole manner had altered. Gone were the fear and unconvincing false bravado with which he'd faced the jury. Heads turned now as, in a loud and carrying voice, he demanded whiskey for himself and his companions, tossing coins onto the bar in payment. The crossed eyes and broken nose were the same, but the drifter no one had given heed to was gone, replaced by someone with the confidence of a man who had notoriety on his head and money in his pocket.

Watching him, Tom Murdock thought, *Where would a man like that get the cash for standing his friends to drinks?* And he felt a crawling suspicion that he could guess the answer.

He switched his attention to McCall's friends, dismissed one as of no consequence, but reacted sharply as he saw that the other was Rupe Barrow, the man who had led the attempt to disrupt Jack Langrishe's opening. Barrow picked up his filled glass and turned to survey the room—and spotted Murdock in the same instant.

The bearded head lifted; Barrow obviously hadn't forgotten that night or Tom Murdock's part in challenging him and turning the scene into a rout. Deliberately, the gang leader drained off his glass and slapped it down. He took a step away from the bar and stood facing Murdock across the suddenly silent room—a bearded, pole-thin figure with a six-shooter strapped around his middle. Then he began to swear at Murdock, insulting him in a flat, steady run of vile language that never rose in pitch but droned on and on, carrying clearly throughout the room and drawing every eye to him and to the man he was foul-mouthing.

Murdock waited it out, feeling his own cheeks go hot with anger. Herb Glennon dropped a hand upon his arm, saying under his breath, "Don't, Tom—he's trying to rile you. Give him a chance and he'll kill you for sure!" But Murdock merely shook his head, pulling his arm away. Without haste, he pushed back the stool he was sitting on and rose to his feet. With deliberate movements, he started toward the other man, who watched him come with a look of anticipation on his bearded face. Like the rest in the room, he couldn't help but see that Murdock wore a gun, but the stage-line owner did not reach for it. Barrow's monologue continued without pause, even as Murdock came to a halt in front of him.

Expressionless, Murdock swung the open palm of one hand and struck the man across the mouth, knocking his head to one side. Barrow staggered, but then he caught himself, drawing up his shoulders. Fiery color leaped into his sallow cheeks.

Murdock told him, "I've had enough of your tongue, Barrow. You're wearing a gun. You want to try and go against me with that instead?"

Barrow appeared to be tempted. His hand jerked slightly toward the holstered gun, but then he let it fall again.

Murdock continued, "You just go right ahead if that's what you want. Pull out your gun, and I'll take it off you again, just like I did that night at the Bella Union. Otherwise, you can just turn around and walk out of here . . . and give us all a rest! We're tired of listening to you."

It was a challenge—with a choice he knew the man was reluctant to accept. Barrow's eyes, red rimmed and furious, glared at Murdock. Suddenly, with a curse, the angry man grabbed for the gun in his holster. Murdock let him get it out, but then he swung his arm at Barrow—this time with his fingers knotted into a fist. The blow struck Barrow squarely on the jaw, sending him stumbling back.

Intending to shoot, Barrow began to raise his gun arm, but his elbow struck the edge of the bar, jarring his hand open, and the gun bounced out of it and hit the floor spinning. Murdock set a boot on the gun to stop it without taking his eyes from Barrow's face. Then in one lightning-quick movement, he drew his own gun and, while pointing it at Barrow, bent forward and snatched up the other man's weapon and holstered it.

The color drained from Barrow's cheeks. His shoulders lost their stiffness, and he slumped breathless against the counter, stunned and suddenly cowed.

Murdock turned to Jack McCall, who stood six feet down the bar, watching as though all this had nothing to do with him. Now, at something he saw in Murdock's face, the mismatched eyes widened slightly. McCall drew a sharp breath.

"Don't point that thing at me, damn you!"

Murdock held the weapon loosely, waving it between the two men. "I'm tempted," he told McCall in a crisp voice. "Since you killed Bill Hickok, you've acted as if you were king around here . . . and there's some in this camp don't like it."

"But you can't touch me! I—I had my trial—and I been cleared."

"Yes! By a jury that was either bribed or scared into it."

"That's a lie!"

"Is it? Maybe you'll tell me this, McCall: Where did you get the money, all of a sudden, that you're throwing around so freely? Did a rich uncle die or something? Or—not mentioning any names—could it be that you were *paid* to murder Hickok?"

McCall was visibly shaking with rage. A pistol was stuck in the waistband of his trousers, but he had better control of himself than to touch it. Instead, he pointed a trembling finger at the weapon Murdock held. "Lay the gun down and say that again," he challenged.

But Murdock simply shook his head. "No thanks. I just thought you should know I'm not the only man in Deadwood who's been asking such questions. Some of those men were good friends of Wild Bill Hickok's. Seems to me you might begin worrying a little. . . ." Giving Wild Bill's killer a crooked smile, he went on, "One thing we've all learned, McCall—it isn't safe for a man to let you walk behind him. But tell me, can you be watching your own back every minute? Think about it!"

With that he dismissed Hickok's killer. Then he drew Rupe Barrow's gun and holstered his own. Opening the cylinder, he swiftly punched the shells out of Barrow's weapon, letting them patter onto the rough pine boards at his feet, and laid the emptied gun on the bar. Turning then to scan the room, he got nods of approval from some of the silent men who had watched the scene. He sought out Studer and Glennon and, seeing them, nodded his head toward the door.

At once the two were on their feet and coming to join him, and without another look at Barrow or Jack McCall, Murdock pivoted around and left the saloon.

Outside, Herb Glennon dropped a hand on his shoulder, exclaiming roughly, "That was just dandy! You took nothing off Barrow—and while you were at it, you told that sonofabitch McCall some things a lot of us have wanted him to hear."

Tom Murdock passed off the compliment. He reminded them, "The three of us were discussing something important before all that. I'd like to go on with our talk. Let's go to the stage-line office. Nobody can interrupt us there. . . ."

Chapter 14

Sid Krauss was trembling as he climbed the hill above Deadwood Gulch, his heart pounding with the effort to appear unhurried. When he had climbed the hill four days ago, after ·hearing Murdock hatch his plan for the decoy wagon, Krauss had been seen by no one on his way up to Varnes's house. But now on the roof of a shack that stood near the top of the steep wooden steps leading from Main Street, a man was nailing up leaks with flattened tin cans. Wiping his brow with his arm, he paused to watch Krauss go by. Krauss was reminded of precautions. Though he was in a hurry, he took the usual roundabout way of approach to Johnny Varnes's house.

Upon his arrival, Krauss was surprised to see Varnes himself step out, closing the door behind him. Varnes planted his fists at his sides and waited for Krauss to reach the porch.

"Well?" he said crisply. "What now?"

"Mr. Varnes!" Krauss gasped between breaths. "I'm afraid they've gone and jumped the gun on us!"

"Jumped the gun—what are you talking about? Do you mean on that shipment?" The gambler's eyes flashed dangerously, and he went on in a threatening voice, "Four days ago, you told me it was planned for this coming Friday."

"It was! They must have changed their minds. This morning, after the stage went out as usual, I had some business across town. I couldn't have been away from the yard more than ten, fifteen minutes, but when I got back, the first thing I seen was the damn wagon with the gold dust, just pulling out."

"What makes you think it wasn't some ordinary wagon?"

"You wouldn't say that if you'd seen the guard. Murdock himself was on it, and Polk Renner and three others—either on the rig or around it on horseback. All of 'em had rifles and sidearms—hell, they looked like a damn army! There was a tarp roped over the wagon box, but I didn't have to be told what was under it. They went on the south road, right out of the gulch . . . and only a few minutes behind the Custer stage."

"And they're still planning to switch the gold to the coach?"

"As far as I know, yes. It's just the day that's been changed."

Johnny Varnes narrowed his eyes. "When did you see the wagon pull out?"

"Must be close to an hour ago, I—"

"And you're only telling me *now*?"

Sid Krauss explained hastily, "I couldn't get away. Faraday had me workin' on jobs around the yard. This is the first chance I could manage." He shook his head with a worried scowl. "I'd hate to think they've caught on to me. I got a good job there, and because of you I could end up losing it."

Varnes showed him no sympathy. "Don't lay your troubles on me. Nobody made you go on the take." He put a hand on the other man's shoulder, then gave him a push. "Now get back down there before you're missed. Keep your mouth shut and your ears open—and look innocent. Don't let on that you know a thing!"

With the air of a man troubled over the situation he had got himself into, Sid Krauss left. Varnes didn't watch him go but, suddenly deciding on a new course of action, went back into the house. He found Creed Dunning staring out the window.

The man turned to ask his employer, "Was that who I thought it was? I been wondering how you always seemed to know what was going on with that stage line."

"Never mind who it was," Varnes snapped. "Can you round up the boys on short notice?"

"Sure, some of them—"

"Then listen! We've got some lost time to make up. All the dust that's been piling up in Murdock's safe during the past several weeks is in a wagon right now on its way to Custer City under a heavy guard. Murdock's being clever: He let it be known he was planning to send it out on Friday, and now he's decided to try and sneak it past me, ahead of schedule."

"Fine! We'll just go take it."

"Wait a minute. That's not all," Johnny Varnes continued. "This wagon is actually nothing more than a decoy. Somewhere out on the trail, the gold will be switched from it to the regular southbound stage. The empty wagon and its armed guards will be left for bait, while the gold travels ahead to Custer. But since we're onto the scheme, we'll simply pass up the wagon with the armed guard and hit the regular coach instead—exactly what they won't expect! It's a cinch," he pointed out. "We're not likely to have another chance like this . . . and there's a fortune involved."

"Maybe you want to come along on this one, Johnny?"

"No, no. You're the one to handle it. You'll have to move fast to catch up with that stage, and I'm not a good enough horseman; I'd hold you back. Just one other thing," he added as Creed Dunning started for the door.

The gunman paused. "What's that?"

"I want Murdock nailed! He's crossed me once too often. He's got the camp so stirred up against me that I haven't dared make a move since Hickok was put out of the way. There's no telling what he'd do after we spoil *this* scheme for him. . . . See that something happens to him."

"It'll be a pleasure," Creed Dunning said slowly. "Consider it done."

He was gone then. Johnny Varnes, watching his man hurry off toward Main Street, was not concerned at all about sending underlings to bring him this shipment. There were some who might be tempted to grab off that much dust for themselves, but Creed Dunning was loyal—and strong enough to overpower the others.

Varnes turned back into the room and went to pour

himself a drink. His hand was on the bottle when a sound, like the creak of a floorboard, drew his attention to the closed hall door. For the first time he saw that the door stood slightly ajar, and his jaw clamped shut beneath gaunt cheeks. He set the bottle down. In two long strides he gained the door and jerked it open—to find Pearl Varnes standing in the hallway, looking at him.

Johnny Varnes stared at his wife, his face a mask of anger. "Well!" he said tightly. "Getting an earful, were we?"

She made no answer; that had come to be the most maddening thing about her—she took his abuse and his rages without offering a word in protest, intent to let him see in her eyes alone the loathing and contempt she felt for him. Now her silence goaded him to fury, and the palm of his hand swept up and across her face in a slap that rang in the silence of the hallway. She didn't flinch from it. The blow jarred her head upon her shoulders, but there was no change in her expression, and she made no attempt to move.

"Haven't I told you," Johnny Varnes said between his clenched teeth, "I will not have you eavesdropping on my affairs?" Pearl's failure to show any sign of fear, even with the print of his fingers on her pale cheek, was maddening to Varnes.

Her appearance ice cold, her voice level, she spoke up to him now—one of the few times he could remember: "I've grown very good at listening. It's taken me a long time to learn for certain what kind of man I married . . . but never before today have I actually heard you give orders for murder!"

This time he struck with his fist. She was sent reeling into the wall at her back. For a moment Pearl Varnes seemed about to crumple to the floor, but she caught herself by bracing a hand against the wall. When she looked again at her husband, there was blood trickling down her cheek.

For a moment their stares clashed. Then, without a word, Pearl turned into her room and closed the door silently but firmly behind her. Looking after her, Johnny

Varnes gave a curse and then, swinging about, returned to the living room and the drink he had postponed. He poured it himself and tossed it down; his thoughts reverted to the news from Sid Krauss and to the all-important mission he'd assigned Creed Dunning.

Suddenly impatient with waiting, he got his flat-crowned hat from the elk-horn antlers where it hung. On the way to the door, he paused to call in to his wife, "I'm leaving now. Don't know how soon I'll be back."

When he got no answer, he raised his voice to add, "You hear?" He frowned. He didn't know what prompted him to turn and cross the hall to the closed bedroom door, but he did, and without preliminary he flung it open.

The bedroom was empty. A bureau's drawers had been pulled out and some articles of clothing flung hastily upon the bed, but in the end she had gone without possessions. An open window showed how she had left.

Johnny Varnes swore again as he strode to the window, ripped aside the curtain when it got in his way, and leaned out. There was, of course, no sign of her. Backing away, he tangled with the curtain again and in furious impatience almost ripped it from its hangings. Afterward he rushed through the house and around it, and finally he stood peering along the hillside at the other scattered dwellings. Somehow he doubted Pearl would have sought refuge at any of them; she had no friends that he knew of among the more substantial residents of Deadwood. On a hunch he started down the hill.

Where the steep wooden steps led down to Main Street, a man nailing flattened cans over the holes in his roof left off work when Varnes called up to him, "Did you see anyone go by here in the last few minutes?"

Kneeling on the roof, the man switched his hammer to the other hand and ran a sleeve across the sweat on his forehead. "If you mean your wife, Johnny—yeah, I seen her going down the hill into town. I noticed because I don't remember seeing her go anywhere alone and without you with her."

Not thanking him, Varnes hurried on. Where the alley at the bottom of the steps led into Main Street, he paused to search for any glimpse of the woman. Not seeing her, he turned up the street toward his place of business—arriving just as armed men were piling into the saddles of waiting horses.

It had taken Creed Dunning this long to collect his crew and for them to get guns and mounts. There were nine horses altogether, worked up and eager to go. Dunning leaned from the saddle of his animal to say, "Don't worry about a thing, Johnny. We'll take care of this."

They looked more than capable. Seeing Rupe Barrow among them, Varnes came to a quick decision. "Leave Barrow here. I've got another job for him." Moments later the rest, with Dunning at their head, went spurring off on their mission, raising dust and a stir of sound that raised curious glances from passersby. After they had passed quickly from sight at the head of the gulch, Varnes turned to Rupe Barrow, who stood waiting for instructions; he looked disgruntled at being left back.

"Do you know my wife when you see her?" Varnes said.

The man gave him a curious look. "Yeah, I think so, Johnny. I've run into her up at your house a time or two. Why?"

"We had a little row, and she's walked out on me. I want her found. She's somewhere here in camp, probably hiding. Take some of the boys and find her—even if you have to search the place house by house. There's five hundred dollars for whoever locates and delivers her to me."

Rupe Barrow looked into his face and nodded quickly. "Sure, Johnny. If she's here, ain't a place she can hope to hide from us. . . ."

"Then get at it!"

And so the search began, descending upon a camp that was already beset by rumors—started, no one knew how—that out on the stage road, on this eventful day, a showdown of some nature was shaping up.

The hunters Barrow had recruited began at the head of the gulch, and they swept down both sides of Main

Street. The armed men trooped in and out of buildings, threatening anyone who tried to hinder them, forcing their way into private quarters or storage rooms or any other place where the woman they were seeking might be hidden. Entering a hotel, they tramped from room to room, forcing the desk clerk to use his key on any locked doors, and roughly booting them open if he refused. Any show of resistance was quelled by the sight of drawn guns.

One shopkeeper who tried to get a gun from under his counter was laid out by a pistol barrel across the side of his skull; cardplayers in a saloon were kept in their places by warning shots into the ceiling above their heads. Perhaps the camp was still shaken by the killing of Wild Bill Hickok and the acquittal of his murderer, for Rupe Barrow and his toughs had their way, almost without opposition.

They found no trace of the woman they were hunting for.

The Bella Union was one of the last buildings before Main Street ended among the cribs of the red-light district and Chinatown beyond. Barrow flung open the street door and entered, three other men at his heels. Apparently no rumor of their coming had preceded them. The theatrical troupe was at work, part of the company seated about the auditorium studying lines or listening while the actors on the stage read a scene from their opened books. When the intruders strode in, the ringing tones of Jack Langrishe met them, rolling without effort through the emptiness of the hall:

". . . and be not so discomfited:
Proceed in practice with my younger daughter;
She's apt to learn, and thankful for good turns.
Signior Petruchio, will you go with us,
Or—"

The voice broke off in midsentence as Langrishe and his people became aware that unwanted visitors had broken in on their rehearsal. Nearly all the male members of the troupe were on the tiny stage, the books in their hands all but forgotten now. Rupe Barrow ran a look over the auditorium and at the curtained boxes, which were obviously empty. No sign here of Pearl Varnes.

Jack Langrishe stepped to the unlighted oil lamps at the front of the stage. Dust specks danced in the bars of sunlight slanting from the skylights overhead. Langrishe said coldly, "What do you want? To finish what you weren't allowed to on opening night? Obviously, you have no sense of propriety at all—you don't hesitate to interrupt Shakespeare himself!"

Something in this man's style and self-control made Rupe Barrow feel ignorant and awkward. Almost on the defensive, he retorted, too loudly, "Forget about opening night! We might get around to that later, but right now we're here looking for somebody."

"Oh?"

"A woman . . ."

"Any woman in particular?" Langrishe murmured blandly.

"Of course, damn you! The boss's wife, Mrs. Johnny Varnes."

He scarcely noticed that he had just blurted full confirmation as to the one who had sent him here, not only today but on that other occasion as well. Jack Langrishe chose not to take it up.

"Mrs. Varnes?" he echoed, tilting his bald head. "Do you mean to tell us she's missing?"

"I'm not telling you anything you didn't already know. You gonna deny you've got her hid out?"

"Of course I deny it!" the other man retorted sharply. "We've seen the lady but once, on the day her husband brought her to the theater—for the purpose of giving himself an opportunity to threaten me. I've heard nothing from her since . . . and the others in my company will tell you the same thing."

"Then you're all lying."

At that, one of the actors strode forward to join Langrishe at the edge of the platform. He pointed an angry finger at Barrow. "I'd like to know what gives you the right to come in here and—"

Langrishe raised a hand against the young fellow's

chest, silencing him with a shake of the head. "Now, Bruce . . . you can rest assured those pistols he and his friends are holding represent the only right a man of his sort is likely to understand."

The revolver had risen in Barrow's tight fist, and he said with a note of menace, "That's for damn sure. And if you don't produce Pearl Varnes, they also give us the right to tear this place apart till *we* find her!"

The young actor had subsided. Every eye was watching Jack Langrishe, who after a moment lifted his shoulders in a shrug. "I could argue the point with you," he said icily, "but under the circumstances it seems hardly practical. You have the guns—and we're wasting precious time. Make your search; if you like, I can show you around. I trust, though, you won't mind if the rest of us get on with what we're doing."

Barrow made a gesture. "Go ahead, for all the hell I care. But we'll do our own looking." To one of his men he said, "Stay here—and watch them." Motioning the other two to follow, he headed for the backstage entrance.

Langrishe managed to have the last word. "Just make sure you don't walk off with anything that doesn't belong to you. . . ."

As they closed the door behind them in the confusing clutter backstage, Rupe Barrow swore fiercely.

One of the others asked, "What do you think?"

"Hell, she can't be here—the sonofabitch wouldn't have been so willing for us to look. But since we're here, we'll look anyway!"

First he went to the rear door for a glance into the alley. The man he had posted there told him, "No one's come out this way." Barrow nodded and, closing the door, looked around at the piles of props and crudely painted scenery, not too well lit by the few dusty windows.

A man and a woman seemed to be alone onstage now, their cadenced speeches coming muffled through the backdrop: "They call me Katharine that do talk of me." And his reply: "You lie, in faith; for you are call'd Kate, and bonny Kate, and sometimes Kate the curst. . . ."

None of it made much sense to Rupe Barrow.

A portion of the backstage area had been partitioned off with a pair of curtained doorways. He went and looked inside. Dressing rooms, he decided; at least that was what they were being used for now. Tables held mirrors and wigs and boxes of greasepaint; a rumpled cot stood against one wall, and garments hung from nails—men's costumes in one room, women's in the other. Barrow saw no one here, either. Disgruntled, he turned away as one of his men emerged from another door at the head of a short flight of stairs. "Where does that lead?" he demanded.

"To a passageway around behind the box seats," the fellow said. "I took a quick look. They're all empty."

Barrow admitted defeat. "Let's go then."

"Go where?" the man asked. "Hell, we've almost run out of places. How long do we keep looking anyway?"

"Till we find her, dammit!"

A silence fell when they emerged into the auditorium. Again, every member of the company stopped what he was doing to look at them, but only Jack Langrishe ventured a dry comment. "I trust you're satisfied?"

Barrow's jaw set, and he felt the heat of anger beginning to spread up from his throat into his bearded cheeks. He allowed himself no more than a glance at Langrishe. A jerk of the head summoned his followers, and he led them from the theater.

That makes twice, he thought bitterly—a second time he had been sent out of there, bested and humiliated. With simmering resentment he left.

Chapter 15

When Rupe Barrow and the other three men were gone, the company stood stunned and silent, staring at one another. Finally someone said, "So Varnes's wife ran away, did she? I guess she could hardly be blamed for that."

Bertie Clevenger had an arm around her little girl, who had not really understood what was going on. Thinking of Pearl, Bertie exclaimed, "The poor thing! That afternoon she was here, she struck me as a nice person but awfully quiet—like she was scared half to death of that husband of hers."

"And with good reason apparently," someone else said.

Ellen Dorsey found her voice. "But where do you suppose she could have gone to? This isn't a big camp. I can't imagine a place she could hide where he couldn't find her."

"Looks as though she's managed so far," Bruce Walker pointed out.

It was Jack Langrishe who put an end to speculation. "In all events," he told his people, "there doesn't seem anything that we can do. And meanwhile, Shakespeare awaits. Shall we resume where we were forced to leave off?"

"I know what *I'm* going to do," Bertie Clevenger declared. To her daughter she said, "You stay with Ellen for a minute. I'm going to have a look at my costumes to make sure those men didn't do them any damage while they were here."

She started for backstage while Bruce Walker and Claire Richards, as Petruchio and Kate, took their places onstage to continue this first run-through of *The Taming of the Shrew*, abbreviated and shaped to fit the requirements of the troupe.

Ellen had never actually read or seen the play before now. She had to admit the two leads looked and performed very well together, though she found herself blushing at some of the lines she heard. She rather wondered if a bunch of miners in a place like Deadwood were going to appreciate or understand it; but Jack Langrishe insisted that Shakespeare always went over well at any place and before any audience.

Suddenly Ellen saw Bertie motioning to her from the backstage doorway. The woman looked pale and upset, and when Ellen reached her, she would say only, "Quick! Tell Jack I want him—and hurry." Then she was gone again, but her urgency had its effect. When Ellen relayed the message, Langrishe asked no unnecessary questions. He laid aside his book, and Ellen followed him as he hurried across the auditorium. She thought afterward that she had known, somehow, what they were going to find.

It was hard at first to recognize the woman who huddled on a chair in the women's dressing room, her clothing dirty and disheveled, her hair undone and streaming about her shoulders. When Pearl Varnes lifted her head, she showed an eye that was bruised and swollen shut and a smear of blood on one purplish cheek.

Bertie Clevenger hovered over her, loosening the collar of the woman's blouse and trying to make her comfortable. As members of the company tried to push into the room on Langrishe's heels, Bertie said impatiently, "Don't crowd her. The poor thing has been hurt. Give her air."

The runaway protested shakily, "I'm all right. . . ."

Jack Langrishe took a step back and stammered, "Good Lord! How long have you been there?"

Pearl Varnes drew a tremulous breath. She had been weeping and was still shaken by her experience. "Not very long." She added, "I could hear Rupe Barrow talking out there. I know he told you I'd left my husband."

Langrishe frowned at her bruised features. "Did he do this to you?"

She nodded, then went on hastily, "I shouldn't have come here. I knew they'd be hunting for me, and I could cause you all trouble. But I—I just didn't know of anywhere else! You people treated me so nice that day I came with Johnny and met you all, I thought maybe you would help me if you could."

"And you were absolutely right," he assured her gallantly. "How did you get in? You must have come through the door to the alley."

The woman nodded again. "But I hung back—I hated asking for help. And then it was too late, because I heard Barrow and his men, and I saw through the window that they had posted a guard. When I realized I couldn't get out, I was too terrified to do anything but hide."

"She was huddled there on the floor," Bertie explained. "Among the costumes. I could hear her crying. If those men had really made any kind of a search, I think they'd surely have found her."

"Oh, my God," Langrishe wiped a palm across his bald and gleaming scalp. "I *sent* them back here! If I had only known . . ."

"If you had, you might not have been half as effective," Bruce Walker pointed out. "They were suspicious to begin with, but before you got through talking, I think you had them convinced they were looking in the wrong place. They likely just went through the motions."

"That may be." The older man sounded dubious and more than a little shaken. "But it was a very close call."

Pearl Varnes insisted again, "I don't want to be any trouble. If they've gone now, I'll be leaving, too."

"You'll do no such thing!" Bertie Clevenger cried. "Jack, tell her she can't. She's safe now that her husband's men have already been here; they've had their look and gone. It makes this the safest place in camp for her. No reason we can't hide her here indefinitely."

"I agree," Langrishe said promptly. "You're welcome to stay right where you are, Mrs. Varnes. For as long as it's necessary."

She looked at the friendly faces about her, and her mouth began to tremble as though on the verge of tears again—but this time, they were tears of gratitude and of sudden relief from terror. "Oh, thank you. Thank you."

"You mustn't even mention it, my dear." Abruptly, Bertie Clevenger was all business. "Now that that's settled, all of you clear out and let me do what I can for that poor, bruised face. I'll need some water."

"I'll fetch it," Ellen Dorsey said quickly.

As the others returned to rehearsal, all of them excited over this latest turn of events, the troupe's newest member got a basin and filled it from the pail of creek water that was drawn fresh daily. When she returned to the dressing room, she found Bertie already at work with the company's medical kit—a necessary item in a milieu as prone to freak mishaps and emergencies as the world of the stage. "Let me stay," Ellen begged. "I want to help."

"That sounds like you," she was told with a smile.

Ellen watched in silence as Bertie worked on the woman's battered features, clucking with sympathy as she gently cleaned away the dried blood and applied a court plaster to the damage from Johnny Varnes's fist. Unable to restrain herself, Bertie demanded finally, "Was there any particular reason for your husband to treat you this way—or only plain meanness? Not that I have any business asking," she added quickly.

Pearl Varnes seemed to want to talk. She said heavily, "I brought it on myself by listening when I wasn't supposed to. This once, he caught me at it. I've never seen him so angry as when he knew I'd overheard him today, making plans against the stage company."

Ellen's reaction was a startled leaping of the pulse. Her mouth had suddenly gone dry. "The Deadwood stage, Mrs. Varnes? Please tell us what you mean."

The woman looked at her, puzzled, and then at Bertie, who quickly explained, "She's trying to say that Tom Murdock is a friend of ours—a real good friend. If he's in for some kind of trouble, it's natural that we'd be concerned."

"I'm afraid it's the worst kind of trouble," Pearl answered in a lifeless voice. "Apparently my husband has found out that they've sent out a big gold shipment today— maybe the biggest one ever. Tom Murdock took it himself—in a wagon with an armed guard. And my husband has sent some of his men to waylay it. I didn't quite hear everything clearly. Something about the wagon only being a decoy. And—I don't know how he learned all this, but I did hear him give the orders, and then . . . he discovered me listening." Her voice broke off.

Ellen was prodded to ask, "Was there anything else you heard—about Tom Murdock himself, perhaps?"

"Oh, yes." The woman nodded, miserably. "Creed Dunning has specific orders, that—that Tom Murdock is to be killed." Suddenly the tears were streaming down her swollen cheeks. "I ought to feel like a traitor, telling you all this—but I can't. Not when I've finally admitted to myself just what sort of man I married. . . . I know now that he means eventually to control this whole area and all the gold that comes out of it. He won't settle for less. Johnny wants it all!"

Bertie Clevenger put her arms around the sobbing woman, talking soothingly, as Ellen, looking suddenly distraught, turned and fled from the room.

Rehearsal was proceeding. When Ellen entered the auditorium, Jack Langrishe called out to her, "Ah—here you are. We're almost ready for Bianca's entrance in Act Three."

She gave him a troubled look. "Mr. Langrishe, I can't. There's somewhere I have to go—something I just learned from Mrs. Varnes. A man's life may depend on it. Please understand!"

"What? What's that?" In the face of her anguish he seemed at a complete loss for words. "Well, naturally. I mean, if—Well, my word!" She was already on her way to the street.

Outside, Bruce Walker caught up with her. "Ellen! Come back," he called, and hearing her name, she reluctantly halted.

"I can't. I'm sorry about the rehearsal, but—"

"Forget the rehearsal! I'm concerned about *you*. Where are you off to?"

"The stage-line office. They simply must get a message to Tom Murdock. . . ."

"But you can't go there, not alone—not in this camp. It wouldn't be safe, even in broad daylight. If the matter is all that important, I'll come with you."

"You don't have to do that. . . . But it *is* important," she added.

"All right." He firmly took her arm. "The office is on Sherman Street, I believe. Come along."

As they picked their way through the press of men idling aimlessly and around those hurrying through the crowded streets, Ellen received some pointed looks. With Walker at her side, however, no one tried to bother her. She was almost too preoccupied to notice. It seemed forever before the stage-line buildings came into sight.

Never having been here before, she looked about uncertainly, thinking at first the place was deserted. But as she was starting for a door marked "Office," someone stepped into view at the wide entrance of the barn. He called, "There's nobody here but me. Can I help you?"

The man was yellow-haired and red of face, a stolid figure in work clothes and a faded shirt. Ellen asked him, "You work here?"

"Yes, ma'am. I'm Sid Krauss—yard manager."

She drew a breath into lungs cramped by her anxiety and her haste. "Oh, thank God! You're someone I can talk to." On the way over she had told Walker a part of the story; now she spilled it all again in a rush and saw the effect on Krauss as he listened.

His expression changed, his color darkening. A thunderous scowl began to harden his features. When she finished, he seemed unable to speak. "You're certain of this?" he demanded finally. "Thing is, the plans for that shipment have been a big secret. I don't rightly know how you could have heard about them."

Bruce Walker retorted indignantly. "Do you think she made this all up? That coming here with it was some sort of joke? If you have any concern for the company you work for, you had better believe what you're hearing. I tell you, she got the whole thing from Mrs. Varnes herself!"

"*Mrs. Varnes?*" Krauss appeared thunderstruck. He stared at Ellen. "When did she tell you? And where?"

"It was at the theater," Walker said sharply. "The Bella Union—she's there now. She had an argument with her husband. There were blows—"

"Varnes hit his wife?"

"*Yes!*" Plainly Bruce Walker was growing impatient at the man's obtuseness. "Yes, indeed—he did a very good job of it. The woman's black and blue, with an eye swollen almost shut. But she managed to get away from him, and she ran to us for help."

Ellen put in quickly, "You won't tell, of course? We wouldn't want anyone to find out where she's hiding. Her husband's already had men there hunting for her. They almost found her, too. And she's terrified." Ellen seized the speechless man's arm. "But what about Tom Murdock? He has to be warned—he has to be told that Varnes knows all about the shipment and is sending his men after it!"

Sid Krauss shrugged off her hand. "It's too late for that," he said harshly. "The wagon left well over an hour ago—and Murdock with it."

"But you have to send a message."

"It's too late. It would never reach him."

"I don't believe that!" She looked around, frantically. "Quick. Let me have one of your horses. I can ride. I'll go after him myself."

But Bruce Walker's hand settled on her shoulder, and his quiet words came through. "Ellen, the man knows what he's saying. There's already been too much time, don't you see? Whatever is going to happen will have happened already. Meanwhile, you did what you could. I think we'd better go back now. Please."

They left Sid Krauss standing with fists clenched at his sides and a strange expression on his face—a look almost of ferocity.

Ellen was silent under a weight of apprehension that seemed nearly more than she could bear. After a few attempts at encouragement, Bruce Walker fell silent also, until they had reached the theater and let themselves into the shadowed entrance. But there he placed a hand on Ellen's arm and turned her to face him. He spoke in quiet and earnest tones.

"You must try not to worry. I'm sure Tom Murdock is a man who can take care of himself. I like the fellow, too, you know." She soberly met his look. "I admire him for what he is and for the job he's doing. The thing is, I somehow never thought of him as a rival. I seem to have missed what was right under my nose."

Ellen shook her head as though unable to comprehend what Bruce was saying.

He placed his hands on her shoulders. "Ellen, I think I understand your feelings better than you do. The way you reacted just now to the threat on Murdock's life told it all. You're in love with the man!" He went on before she could object. "For a while there I hoped that it'd be me you would fall in love with. But I'm glad it was Tom instead. Tom's a steady chap, completely reliable, with a head screwed on right and a strong sense of his responsibilities. Not like me." He gave her a rueful smile. "Everybody knows *my* defects. I'm sure that Jack Langrishe and the other members of the company must have told you that I'm not to be depended on—because I refuse to take myself, or anything else, seriously enough."

She tried to protest, but he raised a hand to silence her.

"I know what they say. And the trouble is, they're right. I am very attracted to you, Ellen, but I just doubt that in the end I could really be the kind of man you deserve. I don't think I'm able to give enough of myself to any relationship. . . . I don't think it's in my nature. Believe me, you'd be better off with someone you can depend on—someone like Tom."

Words tumbled to her lips, but they went unspoken. Looking up into his face, she knew suddenly that what he was telling her came very hard. She might have thought he was simply trying to let her down as gently as he was able, but instead, she understood he was only being honest, revealing what he felt to be the truth about himself. All at once the unshed tears that stung her eyes were not for her, but for Bruce Walker.

"I just can't believe this," she cried. "I know you're wrong about how deeply you can feel. Someday, someone will prove it to you. For your sake at least, I'll always hope so."

Giving her shoulder a squeeze, he smiled and said, "Don't worry about me, Ellen. Or about Tom. Whatever may be happening out there on the trail, you can be sure Tom Murdock's a fellow who knows how to look out for himself."

Chapter 16

Tom Murdock was finding it a problem to keep loose, to ride easily and work the tightness out of his neck and shoulders. It was a blistering day for this altitude. Little air was stirring through the black-trunked pines that stood massed about the stage road. The sun lay on a man like a heavy weight, and insects buzzed in the stillness.

Looking around him, Murdock could tell that the three other horsemen who ringed the slow-moving wagon—as well as Farley Haymes, who sat hunched on the rough seat handling the team—were as tightly strung as himself. Like Murdock they were all well armed; the rifle in each rider's saddle scabbard was oiled, checked, and loaded to the maximum. An extra mount, saddled and bridled and likewise carrying a repeating rifle, followed at the wagon's tailgate. Murdock watched as Polk Renner, riding beside one ponderously turning wheel, twisted around for a probing look behind him.

Nothing showing yet on the trail behind.

Presently a turn took them through a shallow pass, bringing them in view of a bald knob that rose above the timber, dead ahead. Murdock gave this close scrutiny and finally caught a glint of sunlight on metal. A figure stepped into the open at the crest of the knob, a rifle held high above his head. He pumped his arm twice, then twice more. That was Ted Norton's signal, confirming that from his vantage point everything still seemed clear and was going according to schedule.

A quarter mile farther on, Murdock gave the order, and the wagon, under a lashed-down tarp concealing the nature of its cargo, pulled into a clearing ringed by trees.

A swift-running spring, crystal clear over mossy pebbles, made this a natural place for resting and watering horses, and here they found the southbound stage waiting. Its passengers were walking about under the pines, stretching their legs and easing tension while they waited. As Farley Haymes brought his horses to a standstill, the passengers came over to shake hands around. Herb Glennon and Jacob Studer were there along with three other miners who'd volunteered to back up the stage-line personnel.

Any one of this group would have had plausible reasons for traveling to Custer City. George Faraday had managed excuses to avoid selling tickets to any other passengers for this particular run.

Their business here did not take long. In a matter of a few minutes, they had switched heavily loaded boxes from under the wagon tarp to the interior of the coach; in addition to the boxes, they transferred enough weapons and ammunition for each of the stage passengers. While the tarp was being replaced in a manner to conceal any tampering with the wagon's contents, Ted Norton came riding down from his lookout to report no sign as yet of movement along the back trail.

Ready to start, Tom Murdock called everyone together for final consultation.

"We continue as before," he said. "Maybe we'll find that nothing at all is going to happen, but I have too much respect for Johnny Varnes to really believe that. Ted will be positioned between the stage and the decoy wagon as a lookout. Should you run into something," he told Sam Pryor, the coach driver, "we count on him to signal us. On the other hand, if Ted signals you that we're having trouble back here or if you hear gunshots, I want you to pay no mind at all. Understand? Your job is to keep the gold moving, whatever happens; we can take care of ourselves." There was an exchange of looks and nods of agreement. "Very well. Let's move out—and good luck to all of us!"

The volunteers piled into the stagecoach, fully armed now and with the boxes of gold on the floor at their feet. Sam Pryor yelled his teams into the traces, and the coach was again on its way, a fog of dust rising from its iron-tired wheels as it rolled south on the road to Custer City.

Ted Norton, remounted, had a few final words with Murdock, who told him, "You're the kingbolt in this operation. Keep your eyes and ears open."

"Nobody's gonna catch me napping," Norton promised, and went spurring off in the wake of the vanishing stage.

Minutes later the decoy wagon, driven by Farley Haymes and carrying nothing of any value, made a wide circle out of the clearing and turned once more onto the road at its own unhurried pace. With the gold beyond his control now and entrusted to those aboard the coach, Tom Murdock found himself fighting a troubling sense of helplessness. In making his plans, he had considered every possible chance of error and mishap, but a man couldn't help but feel uneasy once things were out of his control.

Presently Polk Renner brought his horse alongside Murdock's; they rode at a walk, hooves plopping into the dust and the bars of hot sunlight reaching them through the towering pines overhead. Renner seemed in an unusually sober mood. "What do you think?" he demanded of Murdock.

"So far, so good."

"I dunno." Renner twisted around to study the road that stretched behind them. Suddenly, he said, "Have you ever had a feeling that all these months Johnny Varnes has been looking right down our necks? That he's known about every single move we made before we made it?"

Murdock gave him a look. "You think somebody's been tipping him off?"

"The thought occurred to me. I've got no names to suggest."

"Me either," Murdock said bleakly. "But even if we *are* dealing with a spy, right now we can only finish what we've started." He didn't have to stress how much was riding on today's operation. Failure to get this shipment through could mean the end of the stage line; on the other hand, success would give them the basis for negotiating a satisfactory working arrangement with Wells Fargo.

They rode in silence except for the creak of leather

and timber and the plodding of shod hooves on the rough trail. Some time later, as though the thought had just occurred to him, Polk Renner remarked, "Say—did you hear about Jack McCall?"

"What about him?"

"He's left."

"Oh?" Murdock looked surprised. "Left Deadwood?"

"Yep. Real quiet, I guess. Fellow named Gus Oberg told me he saw him ride out past Mountain Branch—with all his gear on his pony and looking like he was headed for yonder and no mistake. I haven't heard of anybody that's seen him around since."

"Good riddance. When did this happen?"

"A couple days back, I reckon. In fact, I judge it must have been shortly after the day you raked him over. Wish I could've seen that! I heard you really put a scare into the sonofabitch."

But Tom Murdock shook his head. "I doubt it. All I did was remind him of a few things. Maybe when he thought it over, he woke up to the fact he'd run out his string hereabouts. He could have decided it was healthier for the man who killed Wild Bill Hickok to take himself and his bragging somewhere other than Deadwood."

Not much later than this—when they came to a place where the road just ahead lifted over a spine of tough granite—Renner gave an exclamation and pointed. Murdock had already seen. It was Ted Norton, waiting for them. The barrel of Norton's saddle gun circled in a flash of reflected sunlight, the universal symbol for hurry. Renner said, "I think he's got something he wants us to see."

"I'll have a look," Murdock said, and touched a heel to his horse's flank.

Norton waited, sitting in the saddle, and when his boss joined him, he pointed toward the open land that fell away just ahead. He said only, "Watch! You'll see them. . . ."

It took Murdock a few seconds to make them out. There was timber down there, though not as heavy as on the upward side of the trail—thinned out instead and scattered among boulders. Now a line of horsemen came briefly into the open; sunlight winked from harness metal and the barrel of a rifle. Then timber swallowed them up again as they snaked their way out of the boulder field, but not before Tom Murdock counted eight riders in all.

Without speaking, he turned in the saddle and lifted his hat, waving it in a prearranged signal for those who guarded the wagon. Polk Renner signaled back and yelled something at his companions, and at once they were peeling away from the vehicle, spurring ahead. Farley Haymes, on the seat, kicked on his brake, jumped down, and hurried around to the tailgate, where the extra horse was saddled for just such an emergency. He swung astride and came after the others, and the wagon was left standing where it was, abandoned.

When Haymes and the others joined him, Murdock wasted few words reporting what Ted Norton had spotted. "There were eight of them—enough to tell they mean business. But instead of rising to the bait, they're passing us up and going after the stagecoach. They'll intercept it somewhere up ahead."

Someone exclaimed, "So they caught on! But how do you suppose they could have guessed?"

Murdock exchanged a grim look with Renner, who said, "Nobody guessed. They were told."

"There's no time to settle that now," Murdock said crisply, and lifted the reins. "We have to be moving."

Creed Dunning had ridden these hills enough while working for Johnny Varnes that he knew them as well as any stage driver. Today, calculating time and distance, he picked his spot and pointed his men directly toward it. He avoided the road itself, so as not to risk blundering upon the decoy wagon and its guards. The men he had picked for this job were tough, and so were their horses; they were not afraid of finding a route of their own through rough and untraveled country.

The place he chose to make his play was a steep ravine, rock floored and dangerous enough that a stage driver descending it would be riding his brakes and holding back his team to avoid risking a pileup. The driver would be slowing as he came down that chute, busy with his horses all the way. And when he reached the foot of it, Dunning would be there ahead of him.

The timing was right; there was no sign of a wheeled vehicle having been this way before them. He made his preparations, dividing his men and putting them in the trees at either side where the stage trail leveled after spilling down the ravine. While they waited in the swelter- ing heat, they checked their weapons; presently a murmur of sound disturbed the stillness. The sound swelled, be- coming that of a heavily laden stagecoach and its teams, and then abruptly the coach came into sight and began the slanting run down the ravine.

The man next to Dunning said roughly, "We've made a mistake. Hell, there can't be nothing on that coach— ain't even got anybody riding shotgun!"

Dunning shook his head. Behind the bandanna he had tied around his neck and pulled up over the bridge of his nose, he said, "It's part of the trick. They've put all their guards on that phony wagon—but the trick didn't work."

The stage rolled toward them, brake shoes starting to smoke as the ponderous coach threatened to run down its own horses. By the time it reached the bottom of the ravine, the coach had all but halted, and this was when Creed Dunning and the second rider moved into the road.

Sam Pryor saw the masked faces, the guns pointed at him, and he quickly hauled in his team and lifted both hands above his shoulders, one of them encumbered by a fistful of reins. The restless horses blew and stomped, the sweat and dust plastering their hides. His face grim, the driver swiveled his glance over the pair of riders in front of him and at the others he could see waiting in tree shadows at either side of the road.

Creed Dunning sang out in a bandanna-muffled voice, "You have five seconds to unload your gold!"

The driver answered, "I got no gold. You can look for yourself."

Turning to his men, Dunning ordered, "Go get it. I'll keep him covered."

While one man worked to quiet the uneasy pair of lead horses, others spurred directly toward the coach. Nobody was looking for the revolver shot that lashed out suddenly from an uncurtained window. One of the raiders cried out as he was hit. At the same moment, Sam Pryor tried to snatch up the gun that he had half hidden on the driver's seat next to him, but Dunning caught the movement; he fired, and Pryor was driven hard against the back of the seat.

The raiders had overcome their first shock. Angered beyond caution, they charged the stagecoach now from two sides—and were met by a withering barrage of gunfire out of every window. The smash of gunshot mingled with its own echoes, redoubling as bullets bounced off the walls of the ravine.

Stunned, Creed Dunning saw a man swept from his horse while another, badly wounded, dropped his revolver and sagged forward, clutching at the saddlehorn to steady him. Catching a glimpse of an arm and a hand with a gun in it, Dunning triggered a shot, then saw the arm give a jerk and pull back from sight. His men, though, were giving ground, and he yelled at them, "Shoot the bastards to pieces! Damn you, don't quit on me! There's a fortune in gold in there!" They tried to respond, but in the next breath a frightened horse took a bullet meant for its rider and collapsed, throwing the rest of the horses into confusion.

At almost the same moment, new riders were pouring down from the head of the ravine, and they were yelling and shooting at Dunning and his men as they came. The total surprise of it, catching Johnny Varnes's raiders from a new direction, took what fight was left out of them. All at once Dunning's men broke and pulled away, scattering into the timber.

They nearly swept Creed Dunning along with them. He tried to rally them but was unsuccessful. He got no more than a wild-eyed stare from one man who rode by him, panic showing in a face that bore a streak of blood. Dunning's own horse was nearly wild with terror. He fought it around in a circle, peering through the layers of smoke and dust that streaked the heated air. Suddenly he found himself alone with his enemies.

Then he caught sight of Tom Murdock, and he remembered Johnny Varnes's final instructions: *I want Murdock nailed!* That much, at least, he could tend to. Raising his smoking pistol, he drew careful aim. . . .

He never fired the shot. It was Polk Renner's bullet that struck him in the head and killed him.

Chapter 17

"**T**oo bad it was Dunning I had to shoot," Renner commented sourly. "Maybe we could have made him talk."

Tom Murdock looked at him. "You saved my life; I'll be glad to settle for that. Besides, I doubt that Dunning could have told us anything we didn't already know."

"We still don't know if there really was a spy," Renner pointed out.

"Likely he didn't, either. My guess would be that's something Johnny Varnes would have kept strictly to himself. . . ."

There were more immediate things demanding attention—in particular, their own wounded. Sam Pryor, sprawled limply on the driver's seat, was alive, but the shock of the bullet wound had left him half conscious. Of those within the coach, only Jacob Studer was injured, with a painful, ragged hole in the fleshy part of his upper arm. These two were their only casualties, but they had two wounded prisoners. The rest of their attackers—except for Creed Dunning and another man, both dead—had managed to escape. But they'd gone empty-handed; the cargo was safe.

Murdock sent Art Willard and another man hurrying back to fetch the wagon to convey the hurt men to Deadwood; the bodies of the dead would ride belly down, tied to the saddles of their mounts. Farley Haymes would replace the injured Sam Pryor at the reins of the coach's team, with Ted Norton riding shotgun for the remainder of the run to Custer City.

Murdock spoke to his passengers, whose volunteer effort had turned back the raid on the coach. "I don't know how to begin to thank you. There's no way I could have counted on hiring enough guns to do this job, but between us we may have broken up the gang that's been causing most of the trouble."

Herb Glennon assured him, "We're more than glad to help—it's been our fight, too. If you'll see that my partner gets back and has that arm taken care of, I think I'll just stay with the coach until the gold is unloaded at Custer City. The rest of the boys are agreed—we want to see this thing through to a finish."

"That's up to you," Murdock told him. His own part in the day's work was far from finished, and the pressures on him were mounting. After a few more words of instruction, he turned impatiently to his horse, nodding a summons to Polk Renner.

As they began the return to Deadwood, Renner wanted to know, "Is it your idea Johnny Varnes was one of those who got away from us?"

"Actually, no," Murdock said. "I just can't see him going out on a job himself, not when he had Creed Dunning to send. But sooner or later he's going to learn, or figure out, that things went wrong. And I'd like to get back before that happens. . . ."

Although Johnny Varnes kept reminding himself that it was too early yet to hear the outcome of the raid, this passing of time without any word was growing hard to bear. Waiting for news could breed, even in the sanest mind, the seeds of foul premonition—a sense that when news did come, it would turn out to be bad. Varnes coldly chided himself for giving way to pointless anxiety. Still, as he worked over his business records in the office of his gambling tent, he had to keep himself from getting up and pacing the floor.

When a rap came at the locked rear door, he was instantly alert. The knock hadn't sounded like Creed Dunning's signal; nevertheless, Varnes rose and crossed the room, threw the latch, and then frowned as he saw that the man who faced him was Sid Krauss.

"I told you never to come here!" Varnes said sharply.

"I was careful," Krauss told him. "Nobody seen me."

Varnes motioned him in. Having satisfied himself that no one else was in the alley, he closed the door and turned, scowling.

"I ain't here out of choice," Sid Krauss explained. "I tried your house, as usual, but didn't find anybody. This was the only other place to look."

"Whatever you came for, it had better be important!" Varnes returned to his chair and looked coldly across the table at his visitor. "Well? Something's happening at the stage office? You've had news of the shipment?"

"No word yet. Too soon, I reckon."

"Then what is it?"

Krauss, usually florid of face and unruffled by nature, looked oddly pale and distraught as he gave his answer. "It's Mrs. Varnes. . . ."

This was the last thing Varnes had expected. He stiffened. "Are you saying you know where she is?"

"Maybe. I heard you was looking for her."

"Hell, I've had the boys tearing this camp wide open. If you know something, speak up!" And when Krauss remained silent, Varnes's eyes grew cold. "Oh—you want money, I suppose. Aren't you ever satisfied? Seems to me I've paid you well for selling out the company you work for. But all right." He shrugged. "I've promised five hundred to the one who tells me how to get her back. So far nobody's earned it."

Krauss drew a breath. "I don't want your money anymore, and I've paid you back most of what I owed. I'm not here for that. I'm here to kill you." Then he was holding a gun. His work-callused hand handled it awkwardly, yet there was nothing but menace in the cold eye of the muzzle as it settled on the man behind the table.

"What?" Varnes stared at the gun, then looked up at the white-faced man holding it. "Are you crazy? What is this all about?"

"It's about your wife. She's at the theater. I heard about her from some theater folks who come to the wagon yard to bring us a warning. There was something else they said."

Varnes stared incredulously at him.

"They told me somebody beat her up—used his fists and marked her bad. She claims it was *you*, Mr. Varnes."

Irritated, Johnny Varnes gestured broadly. "Hell, maybe I lost my temper for a minute. I caught her *spying* on me. I'd warned her never to try—"

"You used your fists on her," Krauss repeated doggedly, and his voice was tight. "It's no wonder she run away. I always known she was scared of you. . . . I could tell, the times I used to come to the house. I felt something terrible having to see it."

Johnny Varnes was growing angry. "Do you think I've been paying you to meddle in my personal affairs?"

"You never paid me enough to stand by and see her get hurt. She's a lady, Mr. Varnes! Oh, I know what *I* am. . . . I'd never in the world deserve somebody like *that*. But at least I can make sure she don't have to go back to you when she's scared to. That's why I'm here."

In spite of himself, Johnny Varnes felt sweat begin to break out. "Krauss, don't be a fool!"

"I never killed a man," the other continued as though Varnes hadn't spoken. "But I've got to kill *you*—because I know nothing else will make you leave her alone."

Their eyes met above the barrel of the gun. Even now Johnny Varnes would not let himself show he was under any tension. He drew a breath and said, quite evenly, "Before you make a mistake, there's something in the drawer here that I think you ought to look at." And while Sid Krauss watched, scowling and uncertain, Varnes slid the drawer open and reached inside.

Next moment he was dropping to one knee as his hand came out holding a pistol. Wrist propped on the table's edge, he aimed in an instant. He had taken an unholy chance of having Krauss's gun explode in his face, but for some reason the informant held off the trigger—a second too long. Varnes didn't hesitate. He fired, the sound of the shot thunderous in the little room. Flame flashed in front of him, and Krauss dropped away.

Varnes was standing over the man he had shot, still holding the smoking gun, when Rupe Barrow came bursting in from the main tent. "Johnny!" he cried. "What the hell?"

"He pulled a gun on me."

"Is he dead?" Barrow stared at Krauss, who lay with eyes closed and bloody shirtfront lifting spasmodically with each rasping breath.

"If he isn't, he won't last long." Varnes had other things on his mind just then. He seized Barrow's arm and pulled him around. "Look at me! I sent you to find my wife. Did you or didn't you say you and the boys went over this camp with a currycomb?"

Rupe Barrow stared, uncomprehending. "We sure did, Johnny! We never missed a thing."

"You missed the Bella Union."

"Like hell! We busted in there and held guns on Langrishe and all those theater people while we did our looking."

"Then you let the man make a fool of you again," Johnny Varnes snapped, throwing Barrow's arm away from him. "Because *that's* where the bitch is hiding. If we hurry, we may have a chance of nabbing her." Since he was not wearing a holster, Varnes slid the smoking gun behind his belt. He shoved Barrow toward the open door, ignoring the crowd that stood gaping at them. "We'll pick up a couple of the boys and get down there—before anything else goes wrong."

Ellen Dorsey, as Bianca, was trying desperately to read through a scene with Claire Richards—playing Bianca's sister, Kate—and with Langrishe, as Baptista, their father. But the words seemed meaningless to her; for all her effort she couldn't keep her place or put her mind to what she was doing. Suddenly she burst into tears, dropped the book, and buried her face in her hands. "I'm sorry!" she sobbed, humiliated. "I'm really sorry. I don't mean to act like this!"

To her amazement, she felt Claire's arm slip comfortingly around her and heard the young woman saying, "Jack, I just don't think this is fair. We know the strain she's under . . . and with a performance to get through this evening. Can't you let up on her?"

Ellen lifted her head, blinking through her tears. Langrishe was staring at Claire, apparently as surprised as Ellen herself, and so, Ellen imagined, were the handful of people in the auditorium. Most of the company had been dismissed, but these few—Bruce Walker, Bertie Clevenger and her little girl, and the elderly Hamilton couple—had lingered.

Now Ellen looked at Bruce Walker as she puzzled over this sudden change in the woman she had been forced to consider her only enemy in the troupe. She wondered if Bruce might have been talking about her, telling of her concern for Tom Murdock. That would explain it. It could be that Claire was finally convinced she had been wrong all along, that the new girl was not actually a rival. It might have been enough to remove all her animosity and to let her feel compassion instead for a fellow member of the company who happened to be in trouble.

If Langrishe was startled by the change, he covered it over with an actor's skill. "You're quite right, my dear," he told Claire Richards. "No question that we've all had a trying time today—being invaded . . . and threatened at gunpoint. We'll be better for it in the long run if we let up for an hour or so, relax, put the whole affair out of our minds, and ready ourselves for the play tonight. That is," he told Ellen, "if you don't feel it would be just too much for you to perform. We can still cancel."

"Oh, no!" she cried, horrified at the suggestion. "I wouldn't want that! I'll be all right—I'm sure of it."

"Just as you say." Langrishe turned to the others. "We'll end this rehearsal then. Everyone try to get some rest and a good meal, and be ready to report back at the usual time."

"What about Mrs. Varnes?" someone wanted to know.

Bertie Clevenger answered. "She's in the dressing room—asleep, the last time I looked in at her. Today has been much worse for her than for us, and the poor thing is exhausted. She shouldn't be alone, though, and Cindy and I can stay with her."

"That will be fine," Langrishe said. "She does need someone. I'll send one of the others to relieve you later. Tonight, after the show, I've been thinking we should probably find something among the costumes—a cape, perhaps—that will disguise her enough so we can smuggle her out of here and into the hotel. With so many of us, it's not too likely anyone would notice an extra member in the company. . . ." He paused to look at Bertie for affirmation, and after she nodded her agreement, he said, "Let's be getting along then."

Ellen spoke up, hesitantly. "Would you let me have a few minutes, first? I'd like to see if she's awake yet. There are a few more questions I'd really like to ask—but if she's asleep I won't disturb her."

"Why, certainly," Langrishe said. "We'll wait here. Don't be long."

Pearl Varnes appeared almost lifeless, but her slow and heavy breathing filled the tiny dressing room. She lay on the cot in a drugged, unmoving sleep of exhaustion. Looking at her from the doorway, Ellen thought she might have been quite pretty once; disappointment, and the hardship of marriage to a man like Johnny Varnes, had put their mark on her. But Ellen knew every member of the company was grimly determined the woman should not be forced to return to her husband unless she made the choice freely herself.

Ellen turned away—and at that moment the alley door was flung open forcefully.

Ellen turned, startled. She recognized at once the figure in wide-brimmed hat and fringed buckskins, heavily boned but not tall enough to be a man. The intruder stood in the open doorway, peering around as though trying to adjust to the shadowy interior of the backstage area. "Jane?" Ellen Dorsey exclaimed. "What on earth?" And she hurried to her.

Calamity Jane wasted no time in preliminaries. "It's Johnny Varnes. He and three of his men are headed this way. I just now passed them on the street and heard them talking—Varnes thinks you people are hiding his wife here in the theater. He's coming to find her—and to do I don't know what the hell else, besides."

Ellen stared at her aghast. "Oh, dear! I'd better tell the others—"

But Calamity caught her wrist. "There ain't no time for that. I only managed to get here before 'em by sneaking through the alley. You was real nice to me, that day we met," she went on. "Treated me like a lady. I was hoping I could find you—I'd hate to see somebody like Johnny Varnes get his hands on you. He's mean as a snake. Now come on. We've got to get out of here!"

She tried to drag Ellen through the doorway despite her protests. "I can't! Not and leave Mrs. Varnes—and my friends."

But then, at another glance into the alley, Calamity swore. Stepping back, she slammed the door and threw the latch. "Too late! They've sent somebody around the back way. The fat's in the damn fire. . . ."

Suddenly, out in the auditorium, a trampling of boots and a burst of angry voices proved her right. Ellen froze in indecision. She heard Calamity Jane exclaim, "If I only had my rifle. . . . Dammit, ain't there a gun around here anywhere?"

Ellen shook her head. Galvanized into action, she hurried to the connecting door and swung it shut. There was no latch, only a hook-and-eye fastener that she dropped into place. Calamity Jane snorted scornfully. "Dinky thing like that ain't going to keep anybody out."

Not answering, Ellen Dorsey turned and hurried back to the dressing room where Pearl Varnes lay asleep, looking vulnerable and defenseless on the rumpled cot. A despairing glance told Ellen there was no place here to hide—not this time, not from really determined searchers. She leaned and touched the sleeping woman's shoulder, to rouse her as gently as she could. "Mrs. Varnes! Wake up—*please!*"

Pearl Varnes moaned and stirred. Her eyes wavered open. And then, at what she read in the younger woman's face, her own filled with sudden terror.

* * *

There was stubborn anger in the look Jack Langrishe gave the three men who had dared to burst in on the quiet of the auditorium. Defiantly, he answered Johnny Varnes, "You seem to have been making it a prime purpose to harass this company, from the night we opened. I like to think of myself as a peaceable man, but I have a responsibility to my people, and I can't allow such harassment to continue. I've told this fellow of yours already"—he indicated Rupe Barrow with a scornful glance—"none of us knew the whereabouts of your wife. And it was the truth!" *At the time*, he might have added for strict accuracy, but his tone carried such conviction that his accuser frowned with a hint of uncertainty. "I'll appreciate it now," Langrishe added crisply, "if you will just take these men with you and leave us alone."

They all waited on Varnes then. He stood with arms akimbo, the hang of his coat revealing the handle of the gun shoved behind his belt; Rupe Barrow and the other man already had their guns in their hands. Johnny Varnes studied Langrishe narrowly, then slowly shook his head.

"I've never doubted you were a good actor, Langrishe. And right now you could almost convince me—if I didn't know for a fact you're lying! Come to think of it," he suggested with a faint sneer, "isn't lying your profession? I suppose it's all I could expect, from any of you." But as he looked them over, his eye lit upon the little girl who stood close against Bertie Clevenger's skirt. His expression grew speculative.

"Here, maybe," he said in an altered tone, "is someone who should still be innocent enough to tell me the truth. What's your name, young lady?"

"Cindy," she answered.

"A pretty name," he told her, smiling, "for such a pretty little girl. Come here, Cindy," he beckoned.

Langrishe said sharply, "Varnes!"

The man paid him no attention. After a moment's hesitation, Cindy Clevenger took a step forward, and her mother reluctantly let her go. Johnny Varnes went on in the same mild tone, "Now, Cindy, listen to me carefully.

Sometime earlier today there was a woman came here to the theater. She has a pretty name, too—Pearl. I happen to be her husband, and I'm very much concerned about her. You'll tell me where she is, won't you?"

Staring up at him, the little girl echoed the name. "Pearl?"

"That's right. Now, don't look at your mother," Varnes added quickly. "You just look right at me and answer my question."

The room seemed to hold its breath. Then, in the clear and steady tones of a seasoned trouper, Cindy calmly told him, "I don't remember seeing anyone like that."

Johnny Varnes changed instantly. He stiffened. His bony features warped by rage, he cried, "You little bitch! You're no better than the rest of them." And he cuffed her across the face with his open palm.

As she cried out, Jack Langrishe lost control. He started for Varnes, fumbling at a pocket of his jacket. Rupe Barrow simply raised an arm and pistol-whipped him, gun barrel striking him across the side of the head. Langrishe folded and dropped without a sound. The derringer he had managed to dig from his pocket slipped from his fingers and slid toward Johnny Varnes, who stooped and retrieved it.

"Well!" Varnes commented. "A belly gun. Now who'd have suspected it?"

Confusion had broken loose. One of the women had choked off a scream as she saw Langrishe fall. Bertie Clevenger had caught up her sobbing little girl and was trying to comfort her. And now Bruce Walker, his fists clenched, took a step toward Varnes, crying out hoarsely, "Damn you—"

Johnny Varnes topped all this with his shout, "Shut up—the lot of you!" But it was the guns his men leveled at them that brought silence.

Langrishe was beginning to stir, moaning. "He's not bad hurt," Varnes declared. "You'll all be lucky if nothing worse happens to you. Just don't give me any more trouble." He glanced over at Rupe Barrow, then tossed the captured derringer to his other man. "If they get out of line, I think you know what to do." The man nodded, and Varnes turned back to Barrow. Indicating the door to the rear of the building, he said brusquely, "Come along—show me what's back there. We'll find her for ourselves. . . ."

When Barrow tried the door, it failed to open. "Locked," he grunted. But it was only held by the simple hook and eye, and with a heave of his shoulder, Barrow gave the panel a jerk that ripped the fastener loose. The door sprung open. Johnny Varnes strode through, with Barrow behind him—and halted as he discovered Calamity Jane facing him.

"What the hell are *you* doing here?" Varnes demanded. "You were out on the street only a minute ago." Then it struck him. "You got here ahead of me. You *warned* them!"

"I sure as hell did," she snapped back. "And you're too late. Because your wife ain't here now—she's gone."

He studied her for a moment. He shook his head. "I don't think so. I think you're lying—just like all the rest. Get out of my way!" And he moved to shove her aside.

Next moment it was as though a wildcat had attacked him. Feet and fists pummeled him; a cheek was raked by nails that barely missed his eyes. Varnes cursed and flung the woman off, to be grabbed by Rupe Barrow and with considerable effort somewhat subdued. She was still struggling to free herself, screeching and cursing, after she had been caught around the waist and her arms pinned. Barrow grunted and swore in his effort to hold her.

Johnny Varnes straightened his clothing. "Damned whore!" he gritted. "Get her out of here. Take her and hold her with the others. I don't care how, but for God's sake shut her up. I'll do the searching myself."

When Calamity had been dragged away into the auditorium, Varnes looked about, narrowing in on the doors to the pair of dressing rooms. Not knowing what he might find waiting there, he took out his gun as a precaution. Both rooms appeared to be deserted, but then, on the floor beside a rumpled cot, he saw something that drew his attention. He stooped and came up with a purse, covered with black beads, that he recognized as belonging to his wife. His hand tightened on it; his jaw hardened. He stood listening to the silence.

"Pearl?" he called. Getting no response, he tried again, louder. "Pearl! Can you hear me? I'm waiting for an answer!"

Slipping the bag into a pocket of his coat, he stepped out again into the main backstage area. "*Pearl. . . .*" His voice was a little sharper now. "You know this isn't doing any good!" Looking about for a sign of a hiding place, he saw another closed door, this one at the top of a couple of steps. His eyes narrowed in speculation.

Beyond that door, in the corridor behind the boxes that circled the auditorium, Ellen Dorsey stood with Pearl Varnes trembling beside her. At the very back of the hall were steps that led down to the floor level, but she saw no chance now of reaching them. That insidious voice was coming closer, footsteps were approaching the door. . . .

"Pearl? You're making me angry, Pearl. I don't really think you want to do that. . . ."

With only moments to spare, Ellen turned to the nearest of the boxes, pulling the other woman after her. It was small and dark and contained nothing but three wooden chairs. Past its curtains she could look to the floor of the theater, where she saw her friends being held under the guns of Johnny Varnes's men.

The corridor door loudly banged open. Desperately, Ellen thrust Pearl into a corner of the box and, picking up one of the chairs for a makeshift weapon, placed herself protectingly in front of the woman. Trembling, trying to prevent her own breathing from betraying their hiding place, she waited to be discovered . . . or for the gambler to pass them by.

Chapter 18

Returning to Deadwood, their horses hard ridden and caked with dust and sweat, Murdock and Renner took time to stop at the stage-line office only long enough to ease George Faraday's anxieties. "The job's done," Murdock reported briefly, still in his saddle in the sunbaked yard. "The shipment's on its way—and we're back in business. I think after today we can hold our own, negotiating with Wells Fargo."

His partner was glad enough for even so brief an account.

Murdock added, "Right now, there's something else waiting to be finished."

As he started to ride away, Faraday called after him, "You might keep an eye open for Sid Krauss. I just don't know about him—he's been acting strangely. I left him in charge for an hour, and when I got back, he was gone. I haven't seen him since."

"Krauss . . ." Renner looked thoughtful as he and Murdock rode toward Main Street. "You don't suppose—"

"That he might have been Varnes's spy?" Murdock frowned. "Anything's possible, I suppose. Sid's been a good worker but hard to figure. But instead of making guesses, I'd rather get the truth from Varnes."

"By one means or another," Polk Renner seconded bleakly.

The moment they dismounted before the gambling tent, they knew something unusual was afoot. Card play had stopped at many of the tables, and men were standing around in a state of suspended animation. A bartender saw them and signaled to them. "You're Murdock, ain't you?"

He jerked his head toward the open door of Varnes's office. "You better get back there. We got a dyin' man who's been asking for you."

The two stage-line men exchanged a look, and Renner mumbled, "What the hell?" Tom Murdock led the way. They had never seen the inside of Johnny Varnes's inner sanctum. Right now it was crammed with curious men simply standing by and watching while the harsh and labored breathing of the man they had laid out on the table filled the tiny room. There was, after all, nothing anyone could have done—Murdock knew this the instant he saw what shape Sid Krauss was in.

The yard boss had taken a bullet in the chest, at close range, and he must have been hanging on only by tremendous effort. The sound of Murdock's voice finally got through to him; Krauss's eyes opened, wavered, and settled on the face above his own. Somehow he raised a hand, which then tried to clutch and cling to Murdock's coat sleeve. The dying man's employer exclaimed, "Sid! Can you talk? Did Varnes do this?"

In disjointed words that were barely coherent, enough of the story came out. Murdock listened, incredulous at first and then with growing alarm and anger. There was blood on the man's lips as he finished, in a whisper, saying, "Stop him. . . . Please!" And Murdock nodded.

It was Polk Renner who demanded harshly, "Krauss, how did you get mixed up with him anyway? And why?"

The dying man rallied to answer, "I—I owed him money . . . and he kept upping the amount. Then—then I had to go and fall in love with his wife. . . ."

"I'm sorry, Sid," Murdock told him, and he meant it, but Sid Krauss never heard the words.

Murdock looked at Renner as he straightened and stepped back. "We've got to be going." He glanced about at those who had waited in Varnes's office, curious to see a man die. "Anybody here feel like stopping us?" he demanded, holding his gun hand over his holstered weapon.

Murdock's cold stare put the challenge to a man who stood with a shotgun hooked over his elbow—a man the stage owner recognized as one of the lookouts from the gambling tent. But the fellow shook his head and said flatly, "Not me. I only work here. I got nothing to do with Johnny Varnes's personal affairs."

"All right." Murdock turned and left the office, Polk Renner trailing him nervously through the tent and outside to where they had left their horses. Without a word they unhitched the animals and mounted.

A bull train was lumbering its way down the center of Main Street, nearly filling it—canvas-topped wagons creaking and the slow-moving teams digging up clouds of powdered dust. The need for haste bearing down on him, Murdock chafed over any delay. He managed to find a gap and force his way between a couple of the wagons and, with Renner close behind, went spurring through the traffic down the throat of the gulch toward the dance hall.

The door of the Bella Union stood open. They leaped down, quickly tying their horses to the hitching post. Tom Murdock was already drawing his gun as he strode inside.

The instant he entered the auditorium, he knew he had come upon the scene of a crisis. Some of the company stood like a frozen tableau, confronted by a pair of armed men whom Murdock recognized as working for Johnny Varnes. In fact, the black-bearded man holding a gun in one hand and a struggling Calamity Jane in the other was Rupe Barrow himself.

A look of long-growing resentment leaped into Barrow's face as he saw the stage-line owner enter. He immediately released Calamity, and the woman quickly backed away from him, rubbing the arm he had twisted. Though Varnes's men held revolvers, they seemed wary of the guns leveled at them in the hands of Murdock and Polk Renner. Jack Langrishe stood near Barrow; though on his feet, he looked like a man who had been hurt—his face pale with shock, a smear of blood where the bare scalp had been broken.

Murdock's voice revealed impatience as he approached. "Use the gun or put it away, Barrow. It's your choice. All I want from you is to know where to find your boss."

"Varnes went backstage," Bruce Walker told him. "He's probably tearing the place apart, looking for—"

But then a commotion began in one of the boxes near the stage.

There could be no mistaking the frightened voice of Ellen Dorsey. It pulled Murdock's attention, and despite the maroon drape that half concealed the interior of the box, he was able to glimpse the people inside: A woman was crouched in a shadowed corner, and Ellen stood protectingly before her, a chair lifted in both hands as she defied Johnny Varnes, in tones that echoed through the hall, "Leave us alone, do you hear me? Haven't you done enough already?"

Varnes sprang toward her.

It was with a strength born of terror that Ellen swung the chair at him, but Varnes was too quick and too strong. He flung up an arm to deflect it, and then he seized the object and began fighting her for possession. She struggled gamely, though she was no match for him. After just a few tense moments, Johnny Varnes wrested the chair from her and tossed it aside. Then Ellen was left to face him empty-handed.

Watching in anguish, Tom Murdock raised his gun but immediately lowered it again—there was no way to use it without endangering both Ellen and the other woman. Then he remembered the short flight of steps at the rear of the auditorium that would take him up to the corridor behind the boxes. He was starting to turn back in that direction when the muzzle of Polk Renner's six-gun exploded in a burst of smoke and a flash that was nearly blinding. Through the ringing echoes, he heard Renner cry, "Boss, in another second he'd have plugged you!" Renner nodded toward Rupe Barrow.

Turning around, Murdock saw the gunman reeling and clutching a bleeding forearm, while the gun he had dropped lay useless at his feet. Barrow must have thought he saw his chance; only a quick move by Renner had saved Tom Murdock's life.

Barrow's companion seemed momentarily stunned by what had happened—but not Calamity Jane. With lightning speed she stooped and caught up the gun Barrow had dropped, then spun around and rammed its muzzle into the outlaw's ribs! "Don't *you* get any ideas!" she said sharply. "Drop that!" Hastily he opened his fingers and let his own revolver fall.

Up in the box, the commotion alerted Johnny Varnes. Turning from Ellen, he looked to see what was going on below him and discovered Tom Murdock. Their glances met and held.

The sight of the man who should have been lying dead by now, somewhere on the stage trail to Custer City, must have told Varnes how badly his plans had failed. His gaunt figure twisting, he swept up a revolver.

The two men fired in almost the same instant. Varnes's bullet passed harmlessly over the stage-line owner's head; Murdock's answering shot didn't miss. Varnes jerked violently as he was hit, and reaching out, his groping fingers found the drape that framed the box. They tightened convulsively. The material ripped free, and then Varnes was falling forward, making a slow turn and dragging the curtain down with him as he dropped to the floor of the Bella Union.

He landed in a grotesque sprawl almost at Claire Richards's feet. She stared at him. Her hands flew to her cheeks, which had drained white. She would have fallen in a dead faint had Bruce Walker not stepped forward and caught her in his arms.

Afterward Tom Murdock could never recall how long it took him to reach Ellen Dorsey. He left the prisoners in the care of Polk Renner and Calamity Jane. Carl Mann and his friends—who had come storming in from the No. 10 Saloon next door at the first sound of shooting—were also there to help, and when the man Varnes had sent to guard the back door came bursting into the auditorium, he was quickly taken into custody.

Murdock headed for the steps that led to the boxes. There he found that Ellen had placed Pearl Varnes on a chair and was kneeling beside her, chafing her hands and talking to her soothingly. The woman was white and trembling, but Ellen assured Murdock, "She's all right, really. It's just the shock of having this happen—right in front of her."

He felt there was little he could say, but he made an attempt. "I'm terribly sorry, Mrs. Varnes. I didn't want it that way, but he never gave me any choice."

The woman's head lifted, and her stare settled on him. There was an emptiness in her voice as she said slowly, "Johnny never gave anyone a choice. He wanted everything—and he spoiled whatever he touched. I don't know how he changed like that. I—I loved him, once." And her dull glance dropped to the hands in her lap.

Ellen rose and touched Murdock's arm. "I think the best thing we can do right now is let her alone. . . ."

They moved away a little, over to the railing. They had eyes only for each other. The words rushed from her. "Tom—I've never been so worried as I was about you today. When I learned from Mrs. Varnes what you would be facing, I—I thought I might never see you again. I just don't know what I would have done!"

He could only stare at what he read in her troubled look. His mouth had suddenly gone dry, but he managed to say, "Are you serious? I mean—I know how *I* felt—" He went on quickly, "But I figured it had to be Walker that you were interested in."

Ellen smiled slightly as she looked at her hands. Turning again to Murdock, she admitted, "Bruce Walker is handsome enough, all right, and he has all the charm in the world. But he told me himself that he just isn't the kind of man to form a serious attachment. Although, as for that, I'm beginning to wonder a little now." She pointed to the floor below them.

Murdock saw what she meant. Bruce Walker had not left Claire Richards's side since the trouble ended. He had led her across the hall, where they could be somewhat alone. There they stood with his head bent toward her and his arm around her waist, and he did indeed look more like a lover than someone merely solicitous for a woman who had nearly fainted.

Murdock wondered, looking at them, if in a single

moment of stress a man could all at once overcome his uncertainties and learn at last where his true feelings lay.

During all this there had been considerable activity on the floor of the hall. The stage-line owner was pleased to see that the body of Johnny Varnes had been carried out and that his men were being led away under armed guard. Knowing the temper of the camp, Murdock thought it likely that those unfortunate souls would find themselves being run out of Deadwood without ceremony—and on learning that Varnes was dead, there would surely be others who soon would take the hint and be following. It didn't necessarily mean an end to lawlessness in the Black Hills, but it could be a big step in that direction.

Jack Langrishe seemed to have mostly recovered from being clipped with a gun barrel. He walked over to check on the damage Johnny Varnes had caused to his box drapes, and seeing Murdock and Ellen, he tilted back his head while he spoke to them. He wanted to know about Pearl Varnes. "Tell her, if she'd like people around at a time like this to offer her support, she's more than welcome to stay. On the other hand, if she wants to go home, I'll see she gets there safely."

"We'll talk to her," Murdock said. Langrishe fished out his watch and snapped open the case.

"Just four hours till curtain time. The show must go on, you know. You still think you're equal to it?" he asked Ellen.

"Of course."

He smiled at that—the famous smile that could turn his homely features almost beautiful and win an audience to him instantly. "I shouldn't have to ask! We're very proud of this young lady, Murdock. If anyone had doubts, she's proved herself a real trouper—to rank with the best!" He beamed at Ellen, who was embarrassed but pleased by his praise.

"Well, I have plenty of things to do," Jack Langrishe said, and moved briskly away.

Ellen, still blushing a rosy red, said suddenly, "Oh, look, Tom. It's your friend."

It was indeed Polk Renner, come back from helping

to march the prisoners away. He was seated on one of the theater's benches now, talking earnestly with Bertie Clevenger while young Cindy perched contentedly upon his lap. "They look very domestic," Tom Murdock observed with a wry smile.

"Don't they, though. Bertie was every bit as worried as I was today," Ellen told him. "Only she tried not to let on—but she couldn't hide it from me. Now that it's all over, all I wish is that everyone else could be as happy as I am, Tom—right at this minute!" She slipped her hand into his.

Epilogue

Jack Langrishe never struck it rich in Deadwood. He built his theater, a flimsy affair of wood and canvas, but it probably burned down in the great fire of 1879, which broke out in a bakery on Sherman Street and swept away much of the original camp—including the Bella Union and the No. 10 Saloon, where Wild Bill Hickok was murdered.

It was after this disaster that Langrishe abandoned his theatrical career of some twenty years to go into journalism and politics. He worked on newspapers in Idaho and eventually was elected state senator. In 1890, he died at age sixty.

Jack McCall may have thought he had got away with murder, but after leaving Deadwood, he bragged about it once too often. He was arrested and brought to trial at Yankton, South Dakota—there was, technically, no double jeopardy involved since the Deadwood hearing had been before a wildcat court, without legal standing. This time he abandoned the story about a murdered brother, admitting instead that he killed Hickok for the two hundred dollars paid him by Johnny Varnes. He was convicted of murder and hanged on March 1, 1877.

For the rest of her life, Calamity Jane made a career, of sorts, of claiming to have been Wild Bill Hickok's sweetheart—even going so far as to present herself as the one who captured McCall as he tried to escape from the scene of his crime. When she died in 1903, she got her wish and was buried next to Hickok in the Mount Moriah cemetery at Deadwood. There she lies in her idol's reflected glory, while poor Wild Bill, according to those who knew him, is probably spinning in his grave.

181

As for Captain Bill Massie, the old steamboat man never had the fatal slug from McCall's pistol removed from where it lodged in his wrist. There was too much notoriety in being able to enter a bar, arm held aloft, and sing out, "Here comes the bullet that killed Wild Bill Hickok!"

Coming in May 1984 . . .

STAGECOACH STATION 12:
TUCSON
by Hank Mitchum

Jonathan Dundee and his younger half brother Cooper are locked in
a bitter struggle over whether or not to sell their late father's stagecoach outfit, the Dundee Transport Line—a feud that threatens to
disrupt and endanger the lives not only of their own family, but of
their friends and customers alike. Coming between the Dundees is
efficiency expert Regan O'Rourke who arrives in Arizona with her
young nephew in tow on an assignment to evaluate the line.

Regan quickly finds herself caught in a web of emotions: her
immediate attraction to sophisticated, well-educated Jonathan,
and her equally intense—though far from favorable—reaction to
Coop, who she sees as hotheaded and irresponsible. But when a
plot to take over the stage line results in the kidnapping of her
nephew, along with Cooper's mother and sister, Regan finds she
must put aside her animosity and join forces with Coop in order
to track down the culprits and rescue their loved ones.

Their journey takes them from Prescott to Phoenix and finally to
Tucson, where a final battle will be waged and the final cards
played—and the destinies of Regan and the Dundees will be
decided.

Read TUCSON, on sale May 15, 1984, wherever Bantam paper-
backs are sold.